"I'm Bliss. Bliss Fortune."

The party swirled around them. She held out her hand and as his fingers curved around hers, Shayne felt a sudden jolt that almost made him drop the wineglass.

Bliss obviously felt it, too. Her eyes widened, and when he touched his thumb to the pulse spot on the inside of her wrist, he could feel her heart leap.

"It's the carpet," she suggested, struggling to deny the sexual energy between them.

"Undoubtedly," he agreed, his gaze sweeping slowly over her face before settling on her luscious mouth. What he wanted to do with that mouth...

As they stood there, looking at each other, Shayne had to remind himself that Bliss Fortune was an assignment. One he was determined would end successfully with the lovely lady in some nice federal prison.

His involvement with her would be purely professional. Sexual if necessary. Never anything more...

The author of over fifty novels, **JoAnn Ross** wrote her first story—a romance about two star-crossed mallard ducks—when she was just seven years old. She sold her first romance novel in 1982 and now has over eight million copies of her books in print. Her novels have been published in twenty-seven countries, including Japan, Hungary, Czech Republic and Turkey. JoAnn married her high school sweetheart—twice—and makes her home near Phoenix, Arizona.

Don't miss book III of New Orleans Knights in October, 1997 with MICHAEL: THE DEFENDER

Don't miss any of our special offers. Write to us at the following address for information on our newest releases.

Harlequin Reader Service
U.S.: 3010 Walden Ave., P.O. Box 1325, Buffalo, NY 14269
Canadian: P.O. Box 609, Fort Erie, Ont. L2A 5X3

SHAYNE:
THE PRETENDER
JoANN ROSS

Harlequin Books

TORONTO • NEW YORK • LONDON
AMSTERDAM • PARIS • SYDNEY • HAMBURG
STOCKHOLM • ATHENS • TOKYO • MILAN
MADRID • WARSAW • BUDAPEST • AUCKLAND

ISBN 0-373-25746-5

SHAYNE: THE PRETENDER

1

Paris

BLISS FORTUNE DIDN'T look like a thief. Then again, Shayne O'Malley decided, if jewel thieves actually looked the part, they'd all be in prison and he'd be out of work.

He'd been watching the redhead for the past hour and still couldn't get a handle on her. The way she was working the wealthy party crowd reminded him of a faith healer at a Southern tent revival meeting, and although the French—Parisians in particular—were notorious for disliking everyone, particularly outgoing Americans, her guileless eyes the hue of soft Spanish moss and her dazzling smile appeared to be charming both men and women alike.

It was springtime in Paris. The low pewter clouds that had blanketed the City of Light during the winter had broken up, the famed cool April drizzle was beginning to subside, the chestnut trees were in bloom and life had quickened as Parisians filled the cafés, streets and parks to celebrate the starry nights and sunflower days.

Although women had taken off their wool clothing, the color of choice, despite the season, remained classic black. Except for tonight, when the guests appeared to have pulled out all the stops. The women had dressed in colorful gowns that rivaled the brilliant displays of tulips blooming in the Jardin du Luxembourg.

The party was being held in a luxurious apartment in a seventeenth-century home located on the Ile Saint-Louis, a tiny island wedged into the heart of Paris, between the Right and Left Banks. Constructed to house the aristocracy, the mansions on the island had once been the home to the Rothschilds and Madame du Pompadour. Nearly four hundred years later, it was still one of the city's most desirable and expensive neighborhoods.

Shayne figured there was enough jewelry adorning the party guests to finance another revolution. Gold gleamed, diamonds blazed, pearls glowed beneath the sparkling light of the stalactite crystal chandelier dominating the center of the room. He doubted the Fortune woman would be able to resist such dazzling temptation.

Bliss Fortune had not attempted to compete with the expensive designer gowns that displayed the king's ransom of jewelry to such advantage. She was wearing a sleeveless white silk sheath dress belted low on the hip that skimmed her slender curves and revealed a dazzling length of firm smooth thigh. Contrasting to the simplicity of the little white dress, a pair of very good diamonds sparkled like ice at her earlobes. Shayne wondered what necklace or tiara the stones had been lifted from.

He'd been trailing her around Paris for ten days and outward appearances suggested she was exactly what she'd told the customs agent when she'd arrived on that Air France jet—an antique dealer on her biannual business buying trip. Shayne doubted that she'd missed a single antique shop in Paris and wondered how she managed the energy to check out the competition all day and still shimmer with energy at night. Obviously, she'd never heard of jet lag.

Deciding that it was time they met, he plucked two glasses of champagne from the tray of a passing waiter and made his way across the room.

DAMN, DAMN, DAMN. Bliss couldn't believe it! Of all the parties in all of Paris, why on earth did her rat of an ex-husband have to pick this one to show up at?

She stiffened instinctively as she saw him break off his conversation with an attractive thirty-something brunette and head her way.

"Hello, Bliss." Alan Fortune hugged her as if he had every right to. Which he damn well didn't, Bliss thought as she stood as still as a marble statue in the circle of his arms.

Although the hug was brief, Alan remained standing too close for comfort, his lips curved in the professional charmer's smile that had once, not so very long ago, had the power to melt her heart. Heavily hooded eyes as dark and warm as sable skimmed over her.

"You're looking wonderful, darling."

When he bent his head, as if to kiss her, Bliss backed up two steps.

"You don't have to sound so surprised. I can, on occasion, clean up rather nicely." She was pleased when her cool tone failed to reveal that running into him had stirred smoldering embers of anger she'd believed long cooled.

He ignored her sarcasm just as he'd ignored her temper when she'd discovered him in their bed with a woman she'd thought to be her best friend. Only later had she learned that it was not the first time he'd been unfaithful; discovering that he'd even felt the need to cheat on their honeymoon had dealt a painful blow to her ego.

"I always said you had a natural flair for making the inexpensive appear elegant." He continued to smile as if forgetting that the last time they'd been together he'd been ducking the vase she'd thrown at his head.

Bliss was wondering how on earth she was going to get out of there without creating a scene when the problem was solved for her. A remarkably tall woman, dressed in a strapless gown that undoubtedly cost more than Bliss's car, broke into the conversation.

"Alan, darling," she complained prettily, her smile flashing in a complexion the hue of café au lait, "I was getting lonely over there all by myself."

He laughed at that. "I've never seen you alone, Monique."

The name rang an immediate bell. Monique—and she went only by that first name, like Cher or Madonna—was a supermodel who'd become the darling of the international fashion set. It appeared she was also Alan's flavor of the month.

"Well," Bliss said airily, "it's been nice running into you, Alan, but I'd better go back to mingling."

"That's my Bliss. Always thinking of business."

He was gazing down at her as if she were some rare sort of creature. And that was once the way he'd made her feel—rare and special. Only later had she discovered her workaholic habits were viewed with scornful amusement by him and his circle of jaded acquaintances.

She flashed him a sweet, entirely false smile. "Some of us aren't born with antique silver spoons in our mouths and a fistful of platinum cards in our hands."

She wondered how he'd react if she let him know she'd discovered the truth about his real identity and decided that having to listen to more lies, since he'd undoubtedly deny the story, just wasn't worth whatever small satisfaction she'd receive by bursting his counterfeit bubble of wealthy superiority.

"More's the pity," he returned easily, appearing unwounded by her barb.

Deciding to leave before she destroyed any credibility she might have achieved this evening by cracking him over the head with one of the champagne bottles nestled in the crystal-and-silver buckets nearby, Bliss turned and walked away with as much dignity as she could manage.

In need of fresh air after her encounter, she was standing by the French doors when she sensed someone coming up behind her. She spun around, prepared to tell her lying, cheating ex-spouse to leave her the hell alone and found herself face-to-face with a stranger.

"All that talking you've been doing must have made you thirsty. Champagne?" Okay, so it wasn't the most original line in the world, but when she managed a faint answering smile, Shayne decided it had worked.

"Thank you." She accepted the flute he was holding out to her and took a sip of the wine. The sparkling sunshine on her tongue helped dispel the bad taste lingering from her unwelcome conversation with Alan. "I'm really terrible, aren't I?"

"Are you?" he asked mildly.

"I realize that discussing business at a party isn't socially correct. I mean, even in America. But here in Paris—" she shrugged "—*Cela ne se fait pas.*"

"It may not be done." He repeated the old French expression as he eyed her over the rim of his own glass. "But no one seems to mind in your case."

"Well, they've been wonderfully polite and even amazingly friendly, considering how many rules of etiquette I've undoubtedly broken tonight," she allowed. "But polite doesn't exactly pay the bills, does it?"

He reached out and touched a fingertip to her earlobe. The diamond was a carat, as perfect as he'd ever seen, radiating a blue-white light. "I wouldn't think you'd have to worry about bills."

"Doesn't everyone?" Bliss had to repress a shiver as the light touch felt as if he'd touched a sparkler to her skin. "I'm an antique dealer—I own The Treasure Trove in New Orleans—and in my business you have to spend money to make money. With all the competition, it's important to maintain a high-quality and eclectic inventory, so of course I was delighted by all the steals I discovered on this trip. It truly has been a wonderfully successful trip." Or had been, until she'd had the bad luck to run into Alan.

"Although MasterCard is not going to be at all pleased when they realize how much over my limit I've gone. I've been trying my very best to keep expenses to a bare minimum, but everything is so horribly expensive here, and unfortunately I have absolutely no self-discipline."

Not even enough, apparently to shut her mouth. She'd always been a talkative person and even more so when rattled. Which she definitely was at the moment, with those steady pale blue eyes looking so deeply into hers.

"Did you know that Hemingway, when he lived in Paris, actually wrote about having a 'high grade' dinner for two, with wine, for only twelve francs?"

"I don't think I've ever heard that."

"Well, he did. Of course today, a simple cheese sandwich costs nearly three times that."

He saw her cast a covetous glance toward the damask-draped buffet table, decorated with candelabra and offering enough food to feed Napoleon's armies.

"They seem to have put out a pretty nice spread here," he said.

"They have, haven't they? I'm afraid if I began filling a plate, I'd end up eating like a long-haul truck driver." Her sigh ruffled her curly red-gold bangs. "French women never eat, of course. You always see them sitting looking so elegant in the sidewalk cafés with plates in front of them, but you never see them actually take a bite. I firmly believe that it's against the law."

Her gaze briefly circled the room and returned to the table groaning with delicacies. Another sigh. "Even so, I could kill for a steak right about now."

"Why don't we pile some stuff on my plate?" he suggested. "You can stick to a nice, ladylike piece of cheese or fruit, then we'll go out onto the terrace and you can eat all you want without anyone noticing."

She smiled up at him and it crossed his mind again that if he didn't know better, he would believe this blithe spirit had not an ounce of guile.

"That's so sweet of you. And honestly, I'm not usually such a mooch, but I've had hardly anything to eat since yesterday—you'd think I was in the Bastille, for heaven's sake—and I'm absolutely starving." She stopped for a moment. "Do you know, I have absolutely no idea why I'm telling you this. In fact, I don't even know who you are."

"I'm Shayne Broussard." It was his mother's maiden name. And although it was technically Cajun, not French, it worked well enough in this setting.

"I'm Bliss. Bliss Fortune." She held out her hand and as his fingers curved around hers he felt a sudden jolt that almost made Shayne drop the wineglass he was holding in his free hand.

She obviously felt it, too. Her eyes widened and when he touched his thumb to the pulse spot on the inside of her wrist he could feel her heart leap.

"It's the carpet," she suggested, struggling to deny this newfound scientific evidence that sexual energy could be measured in megawatts.

"Undoubtedly," he agreed, his gaze sweeping slowly over her face before settling on her mouth.

As they stood there looking at each other, Shayne had to remind himself that Bliss Fortune was an assignment. One he was determined would end successfully, with the lovely lady landing, not exactly in the Bastille, but some nice federal prison back in the States.

"Ready to eat?"

The intimacy in his eyes was suggesting something else all together. Reminding herself that men and women routinely flirted in Paris, that it was, after all, the French who'd given the world the phrase *le coup de foudre*, love at first sight, Bliss decided to enjoy the fact that such a gorgeous man found her appealing.

"Absolutely."

Shayne glanced across the room to the man who'd embraced her earlier. "Not that I want to warn you away, but what about your friend?" he said, as if it were an afterthought.

"Friend?" She followed his gaze. "Oh. Alan. He's certainly not a friend. Merely a ghost of an old marriage past."

"Ah." He nodded understandingly. "I see."

"How nice one of us does," she responded dryly.

Having had plenty of time to think about what in the world she'd ever seen in Alan Fortune in the first place, she'd come to the conclusion that the problem had been she hadn't been seeing clearly at all. Instead, she'd allowed herself to be blinded by the bright and shining aura of the man she'd thought him to be.

Deciding not to ruin her successful shopping trip by contemplating her short, ill-fated marriage, she headed off toward the table, Shayne behind her.

He didn't feel a single iota of guilt for enjoying the sway of her hips in that short white dress. Cunningham had told him to watch Bliss Fortune. And that's just what he was doing. Some duties, he decided, as Bliss reached for a gilt-rimmed plate, causing the dress to rise even higher, were definitely more appealing than others.

The night was cool and tinged with the scent of distant rain. As they took their plates out onto the terrace, Shayne noticed her slight shiver.

"Here." He took off his suit jacket and put it over her shoulders. "Can't have you catching pneumonia. If you think the food's expensive, imagine what a doctor would charge for a house call to your hotel."

"I don't even want to think about it." She settled down in a wrought iron chair, took a mussel from his plate, popped it into her mouth, closed her eyes as she chewed and nearly swooned. "I think I've just died and gone to heaven."

"They're *moules brûles doigts*, otherwise known as burn-your-fingers mussels. They're kept in salted water, then put on a super hot iron plaque which steams them open and concentrates the sweetness."

"What they are is heaven." She plucked another one from the plate and devoured it.

Watching her, Shayne wondered idly if she could receive such ecstasy from a mere mussel, what she'd be
like in the throes of orgasm.

"How do you know that?" she asked when she finished chewing.

He pulled himself out of the unbidden fantasy of
watching that silk dress slide down her body. "Know
what?"

"About mussels. Are you going to eat that cheese?"

"Be my guest." He put his plate in front of her and
leaned back in his chair. "I enjoy cooking. I find it relaxing. I took a class a few years ago at the Cordon Bleu and
picked it up there."

Bliss stopped in the act of spreading the soft Camem-
bert over a piece of crusty bread. "You've actually taken
classes at the Cordon Bleu cooking school?"

He shrugged. "I told you, cooking relaxes me. And I
figured if I was going to tackle French, I might as well
learn from the best."

"No argument there." She took a bite, savoring the
cheese with the same pleasure as she had the mussel. "I
suppose you chose French because of your ancestry. You
are American, right?"

"Right. And I chose French because I viewed it as a
challenge."

"And you enjoy challenges."

"I live for them."

"Me, too. Lately I've had a few more than I'd prefer,
but life would be incredibly boring without its little
tests, wouldn't it?"

"That's what they say."

Shayne decided that whichever parent had decided to
name her Bliss had chosen well. The woman seemed to
find delight in the simplest of things. Once again he

thought she was the unlikeliest felon he'd ever met. Then reminded himself of how well she'd worked that room and decided that she was a lot slicker than she appeared.

"Are you rich?"

The directness of the question caught him by surprise. "Would it matter?" he asked, taking another drink of champagne and idly wishing it was a beer. A nice cold Dixie with beads of moisture running down the long neck of the bottle.

One of the problems with playing this role of the international jet-set playboy was that it kept a guy from enjoying the simpler pleasures in life. Like a cold beer on a hot summer afternoon, a hot dog at the ballpark, a day of crawfish trapping in the bayou.

An uncharacteristic feeling that resembled homesickness tugged at chords deep inside him. As he always did under such circumstances, Shayne ignored it.

"It's just that I was really beginning to like you," Bliss explained. "After all, it's not every man who'd share his *moules brûles doigts* with a total stranger. But I have a rule about getting involved with rich men."

"I'd think that your business would depend on wealthy individuals." After all, Shayne considered, you couldn't make all that much money stealing jewels from the poor. "And are we getting involved?"

"I've always tried to separate business from pleasure. As for getting involved, well, no, I suppose we're not," she admitted with a quick, somewhat abashed grin. "But we might have been." She stood up and held out her hand again. "Good night, Mr. Broussard. It's truly been a pleasure."

He took the slender hand in both of his. "You're not leaving before dessert?"

"I'm sorry." Her cap of bright curls bounced as she shook her head. "I told you, I have a rule against getting involved with wealthy men."

"We don't have to get involved."

"But that's the problem you see—" her green eyes became earnest "—I told you, I have no self-discipline. Well, actually, I do, at least when it comes to important things like my business and voting and paying my taxes and not littering, but I've always tended to be horrendously impulsive in my personal life, and since I'll admit to having been attracted to you from the minute you walked in the door—"

"I hadn't realized you'd noticed me."

"It's difficult not to notice a devastatingly goodlooking man who doesn't take his eyes off you," she answered.

"You were the most appealing sight in the room." He glanced over at the river, where a *bateau-mouche* was passing by, lit up like Bourbon Street back home in New Orleans. "You know, you really haven't seen the City of Light until you've seen it from the river. Come for a boat ride with me, Bliss. You'll be surrounded by tourists who can act as bodyguards and if it'll make you feel safer, I promise to keep my hands in my pockets at all times."

Damn. He'd hit on the one thing that was so, so tempting. The boats were one of the most enticing experiences Paris had to offer. She remembered once coming to the city with Alan, who'd refused her entreaties for just such a ride, proclaiming them a floating cliché. Which they might well be, but that didn't stop her from loving the idea of them.

Bliss gave him a long considering look. Although she'd been drawn to him the minute she'd seen him, leaning up against that silk-draped wall watching her with unwavering intensity, she'd made the decision to walk away from temptation.

Absolutely nothing had changed in the last few minutes; Shayne Broussard was too charming, too smooth, too confident. And, too rich, Bliss reminded herself.

"I'm sorry," she said again. "I just know that no matter how honorable your intentions, I'd end up letting myself get involved with you, and then..." She shrugged. "There you go."

"Go where?"

"Checking into the Heartbreak Hotel." This time her smile was unmistakably wistful, reminding him of a starved waif staring in a bakery window at a tray of chocolate éclairs. "I truly do believe that it's better if I leave now. Before things get complicated."

That said, she withdrew her hand gently from his, slipped the jacket from her shoulders and put it over the back of her abandoned chair, then returned to the party.

Shayne stood up, walked over to the French doors and watched as she disappeared into the bedroom where the coats had been collected.

He cursed. Then laughed. "So much for the old Broussard charm." Since he'd taped a microphone to his body before getting dressed for the party, he knew that somewhere in the city his superior would be listening to their conversation and laughing his head off.

Shayne tilted his head in an almost imperceptible nod toward a woman standing beside the buffet table. She nodded back, then went into the bedroom as well to cover their target while Shayne left the building.

"What a lovely wrap."

Bliss smiled at the forty-something woman who'd just

plucked a mink coat from the bed. "Thanks." She shrugged into the red satin baseball jacket in question. "It's not really appropriate for this type of party, I suppose, but I believe in traveling light."

"That's wise." The woman, who epitomized elegance, smiled back.

As they stood there, looking at one another, Bliss had the feeling she was expected to say something. "Are you an American?"

"From Seattle," the woman lied blithely. "But I've been living in Paris for the past ten years. Did I hear you tell someone that you're an antique dealer?"

"Yes." Ever ready, Bliss took a business card out of her purse. "If you're ever in New Orleans, drop in and say hi."

"I just may do that." The woman slipped the card into her ivory satin bag without looking at it. "Are you going to be in the city long? Perhaps we can have lunch."

"I'm leaving in the morning."

"Ah." A penciled brow lifted. "Then you've concluded your business successfully, I presume?"

"Not really." Bliss shrugged and tried not to sigh. "But I've left my shop too long as it is." Zelda, who'd promised to help out during her absence, had probably given away half the stock by now. Her beloved grandmother, while appreciating fine things, had never been known for her business sense.

"Well then, have a safe flight home. And if I ever visit your city, I'll be sure to look you up."

"I'd like that." Bliss returned the smooth smile with a quick one of her own, then left the bedroom.

She should have taken a few rolls with her, she thought as she waited for the elevator. It would have saved having to buy something to eat at the airport while waiting for her flight. Unfortunately, her meeting with Shayne Broussard had left her feeling more than a little distracted.

He certainly seemed nice, although really, when you thought about it, why shouldn't wealthy people be nice? When you weren't worried about mortgage payments and power bills and trying to figure out a new way to stretch ground turkey, you'd certainly have less reason to be stressed-out and snappish.

Alan had certainly seemed nice enough. In the beginning. And Shayne Broussard was every bit as smooth as her ex-husband. And even more handsome. In fact, she thought as she stepped into the old-fashioned cage elevator, she'd never met such a good-looking man.

His hair was as black as midnight, his eyes as blue as a summer sky. The contrast was riveting enough even before you tacked on that gorgeous straight nose, those chiseled lips and teeth so perfect that if they hadn't been professionally straightened was even more proof that life was decidedly unfair.

He was tall. She was five foot six, and she'd had to tilt her head back to look up at him. His deep tan suggested he spent a great deal of time in the sun, undoubtedly lounging around on topless beaches in the south of France and his body, beneath the Italian custom-tailored suit and silk shirt, appeared lean and hard.

"I wonder if he works out," she murmured.

No. She couldn't imagine him sweating in some common gym. It was easier to picture him playing polo, fencing or skiing at some jet-set gathering place in the Alps.

"He's not for you," she reminded herself firmly as the elevator reached the ground floor. "You've had your fling with the rich and famous. And paid for it, big time."

The first three months of her marriage—along with her brief whirlwind courtship—had been the most exhilarating time of her life. She and Alan had honeymooned on a yacht in the Greek Islands, made love in a high feather bed in Provence, hung out with movie stars at the Cannes film festival and just before everything had fallen apart, they'd attended a dinner party in SoHo where John Kennedy Jr. and Madonna had both shown up—although not together.

Life had seemed like a continual costume ball and she'd felt like Cinderella. Unfortunately, she'd never realized that come midnight her Prince Charming would turn into a rat.

2

As she came out of the building, Bliss found Shayne waiting for her. She was not all that surprised. She was, however, more than a little unnerved at the warmth of pleasure that flowed through her at the sight of him.

"So," he greeted her, as if she hadn't cut the conversation off so abruptly upstairs, "how much would it take?"

Bliss eyed him warily. Despite his easygoing behavior, she sensed a steely core that made her suspect this man could be extremely hazardous to a woman's emotional health.

"How much what?"

"How much money would I have to give away before you agreed to have dessert with me?"

"I told you—"

"I know." Without waiting for an invitation, he fell into step with her as she began walking away. "You don't get involved with rich guys. And I don't know what's happened to make you so down on an entire group of the world's males, but don't you think that behavior's a little rigid? Especially for Paris?"

The *tap tap tap* of her high heels on the cobblestone sidewalk reminded Bliss that being alone at night in a foreign country with a total stranger was definitely one of the riskier things she'd ever done.

"That's partly my point," she answered, knowing that

if she looked up at him and viewed the smile she heard in his voice that she'd have trouble sticking to her guns. "Paris is precisely the kind of city where people have flings."

"So now you're against flings with rich men, too? I thought it was just involvement you were determined to avoid."

She stopped beneath the spreading yellow glow of a streetlight and looked up at him. "Are you always this impossibly stubborn?"

"When I want something badly, yes."

Well, that was certainly to the point, Bliss decided, reluctantly giving him points for honesty. "And you want me?"

"Sweetheart, a man would have to be stone-cold dead for a month of Sundays to not want you. However, at the moment I'm willing to settle for a walk along the river, perhaps share a few pastries, and pass the time in friendly, getting-to-know-you conversation."

"And if I don't want to get to know you?"

He laughed, the sound streaming through her like warm summer sunshine. "Of course you do. The same way I want to get to know you. I'll make you a deal."

"The last time someone said that to me, I ended up buying a fake Meissen shepherdess."

"I'm not selling any counterfeits today," he lied deftly.

The truth was, of course, that his entire story was a fake. Hell, his whole life these past years was a tangled web of lies, when you got right down to it. It was getting so even he had trouble keeping track of who he was, Shayne thought, a bit disgusted with himself. But not enough to tell her the truth. She was, after all, he reminded himself firmly, a consummate liar herself.

"It's just that I'm in a strange mood tonight," he said. Now that much was the truth. "I don't feel like being alone."

"Now that's encouraging," she muttered. "Personally, I think the champagne remark was a better pickup line. If you're accustomed to mentioning strange moods when you're with a woman on a dark street it's no wonder you're alone."

He laughed again. Again she found it unnervingly charming. "You have a point. So, how about we get off this dark street and go somewhere public?"

She really shouldn't. For some reason—perhaps it was his black Irish looks—this man reminded her of her tenant, Michael O'Malley. She could just imagine what the former homicide cop turned private investigator would say about her incautious behavior. He would undoubtedly hit the roof.

"What did you have in mind?" she heard herself asking.

"I believe I mentioned a boat ride."

Once again it was so, so tempting. "You promised to keep your hands in your pockets," she reminded him.

"Absolutely," he lied again as he dipped them into the pockets of his gray slacks.

Twenty minutes later, sitting on the upper deck of a boat gliding slowly down the Seine, with a backdrop of the Eiffel Tower glistening like an oversize Christmas tree, Bliss realized that she'd made an error. This was more than just a tourist cliché, like the Mad Hatter's teacup ride or the Matterhorn at Disneyland. Despite the fact that the boat was crowded with people rattling away in a dozen different languages, this was, without a doubt, the most glamorous and romantic experience of her life.

The lights of the boat created a shimmering silver veil over the water and cast the magnificent Gothic arches of Notre Dame in a dramatic brilliance. It reminded Bliss of the first time she'd experienced the aurora borealis while vacationing in Maine. Dazzling and magical and something she knew she'd remember vividly for the rest of her life.

"You're suddenly awfully quiet." He turned toward her, leaned across the small table between them and toyed with a curl that the spring breeze had brushed against her cheek.

The night air was cool; his fingers felt like a touch of flame against her skin. And Bliss knew that she was sunk.

"I was just thinking that perhaps this isn't such a bad way to end my time in Paris," she murmured.

He smiled at that. A bold, confident smile that should have made her hate him but unfortunately held so much charm she couldn't even muster up a decent dislike. "Does this mean you're rethinking your position on wealthy men?"

"No." On this she was firm. Before Alan, she'd always prided herself on standing on her own two feet. Now that she was on her own again, the ground beneath her feet might be a little unstable, but she'd survive it. As she'd survived so much else in her past. "But it does mean that perhaps I'll suspend judgment. Just for tonight."

"Tonight's a beginning." He took her hand, linked their fingers together and gave her another of those slow perusals that warmed her blood and made her pulse race. "You really are stunning."

"Of course." Her cool smile was designed to conceal

another attack of nerves. "It is Paris, after all. All women appear stunning at night in Paris."

"I know I promised to surround you with body-guards," he said as the boat pulled over to pick up a group of Japanese tourists, "but how would you feel about walking for a while?"

Throwing the last remaining bit of caution to the wind, she stood up. "I'd like that."

Bliss reminded herself that this was Paris and, after the year she'd had, she deserved a little fling. Besides, it was growing late and in the morning she'd be back on the plane to the States. What could happen in a few short hours?

They strolled along the Left Bank, passing lovers em-bracing in doorways and a saxophone player sending sad, lonely notes against the stone walls. They stopped and bought ice cream from an elderly vendor who in-sisted Bliss was truly the most beautiful woman in all of the city, then later, when the April drizzle began again, they laughingly ducked into a bistro where they drank glasses of white house wine that tasted like buttered sunshine.

After the rain, they continued along the cobblestone streets, stopping again when Shayne insisted that she have her portrait painted by an artist who'd set up shop on the sidewalk. A crowd of American tourists began to gather, and although Bliss was a bit uncomfortable be-ing the center of attention, she had to admit that she was flattered by both the flirtatious comments of the artist and the final results.

"Now you," she said, getting up from the stool so Shayne could take his turn.

"I don't think so," he said, smiling. He'd become an

expert at never having his picture taken. In his business even a pastel chalk likeness would be a mistake.

"But…"

Not wanting to get into an argument, but realizing that she was not going to surrender easily this time, he did the first thing that popped into his mind. He bent his head and kissed her.

The touch of his mouth against hers only lasted an instant. But it was still long enough to cause her breath to back up in her lungs and needs she'd forgotten she possessed to slice through her. His lips were cool; the emotions they stirred were anything but.

"What was that for?" she asked, shaken but loath to show it.

Those chiseled lips she could still taste curved upward in an outrageously attractive, unrepentant grin. "It's Paris," he said, as if that explained everything.

Which, Bliss decided, it undoubtedly did.

"You promised to keep your hands in your pockets."

"I did."

She heard the sound of change jangling as proof and realized that he was telling the truth. So why was it that for that fleeting second she'd imagined she could feel his hands touching her everywhere?

"I knew this was a mistake," she murmured.

"It was only a kiss."

"True."

Although she hadn't wanted him to kiss her in the first place, Bliss was annoyed by the way he so easily dismissed something so mind-blinding. She also wondered briefly how many women he'd kissed while strolling along this same river. How many women he'd taken into his arms in some out-of-the-way garden? How many he'd made love to.

"You're right, of course." He took his left hand from his pocket and rubbed at the line etched between her coppery brows with the tip of his index finger. "Technically, I cheated. But I'm afraid I enjoyed it too much to apologize."

His easy words reminded her that he was a man accustomed to getting his way. A rich man.

"I really should be getting back to my hotel," she murmured. "I still have to finish packing before my flight."

"I don't suppose you could change your flight?"

When that treacherous finger began trailing down the side of her face, heating her skin, Bliss backed away. "No. I can't."

She'd expected an argument, but once again he surprised her.

"Whatever you want."

Shayne summoned a taxi and they sat side by side in the back. Neither said a word. But the sexual tension was strung so strongly between them Bliss felt she could reach out and touch it. Instead, she kept her hands clasped together tightly in her lap, her gaze directed steadfastly away from him, out the window.

When the taxi arrived at her hotel, she expected another argument about whether or not he'd accompany her upstairs, but he seemed content to merely walk her to the door.

"Thank you for a lovely evening. And, although I know this will sound like a horrendous cliché, I'll enjoy knowing that we'll always have Paris."

That said, he lifted her hand to his lips. Then gave her another of those heart-melting smiles and walked away.

She entered the lobby, but unwilling to completely surrender the magic of the evening, Bliss stood by the window, watching the taxi drive away.

When the taillights disappeared around a corner, she sighed. Then went back upstairs to finish packing for her trip home to New Orleans.

"WHAT THE HELL do you mean, she did it again?"

Two days after meeting Bliss Fortune, Shayne O'Malley was pacing the floor of his superior's office, frustration and disbelief radiating from every pore.

"The diamond-and-sapphire earrings we'd left in a jewelry box in the bedroom disappeared after Ms. Fortune retrieved her coat," David Cunningham revealed.

Shayne's curse was ripe and vicious. "That's impossible."

"Apparently not."

"I watched her the entire time."

"I know." Cunningham's smile reminded Shayne of a rattler. "I haven't yet congratulated you on coming up with a way to take her mind off having your portrait painted. That kiss was inspired.

"And isn't it admirable," he continued, his voice laced with the acid sarcasm Shayne had learned to expect from the older man, "what sacrifices a man is willing to make for his country."

The memory of the brief kiss flooded back. It had been a mistake. But one Shayne couldn't regret. "You told me to watch her."

"And you did. Admirably."

Again the sarcasm stung. Again, Shayne managed, just barely to keep from commenting and returned his thoughts to this latest glitch in the investigation.

"I don't get it." He raked his hand through his hair and resumed pacing again. "Gwen followed her into the bedroom. Between the two of us, there wasn't a time when Bliss Fortune was alone long enough to steal anything."

"Although I hate to admit it, the woman's a master thief," Cunningham said. "Fortunately, the jewels in question were paste. Very good paste," the older man qualified. "Which means that your screwup has still cost the government a great deal of money."

"I don't get it," Shayne repeated as he glared out at the Louvre's glass pyramid. How the hell could she have done it? He was the best. Nobody outfoxed Shayne O'Malley.

"Washington's losing patience." Cunningham's voice broke into Shayne's thoughts. "The guys at Interpol are laughing at us for not being able to apprehend a mere woman. You need to stop Bliss Fortune, O'Malley. Now."

"What do you expect me to do?" Shayne shot back. "Go to New Orleans, lock her in her precious antique shop, shine bright lights in her face and beat her with a rubber hose until she confesses?"

"Whatever it takes," his superior said mildly. But the steel in his gray eyes assured Shayne that the instructions were no exaggeration.

3

New Orleans

THE CIRCUMSTANCES WERE not what Shayne would have chosen. A full white moon floated like a galleon in the night sky, casting a bright light on New Orleans's French Quarter. He would have preferred the sheltering cover of darkness; after all, when you were breaking into a building, the one thing you didn't want was a damn spotlight shining down on you.

But unfortunately in his business, you often had to work under less than optimum conditions. So rather than complain, he set to work, opening the door with a mere flash of the steel pick. Once inside he turned on the flashlight. The silent alarm proved no problem; he suspected a twelve-year-old hacker could disengage it in a matter of minutes. It took Shayne less then ten seconds.

He locked the door behind him, then, not daring to turn on the lights, circled the room with the yellow flashlight beam.

For someone who'd chosen to live life on the edge, Shayne was a stickler for order wherever he could find it. One quick glance assured him that he wasn't going to find it here.

Bliss Fortune's beloved Treasure Trove was a jumble of mismatched merchandise, offering everything from an exquisitely carved mahogany cockfighting chair to a porcelain statue of Buddha to the collection of army helmets on a shelf above a gesso-painted wooden sarcophagus. If it hadn't been for the helmets and the sarcophagus, the place would have reminded him of his grandmother Broussard's attic.

It was not going to be easy, locating those earrings, he considered, flashing the light over the locked display case of stuffed animals. But Shayne had suffered enough close calls that he'd learned not to trust in easy. Actually, with very few exceptions, he never trusted anything or anyone. Which was why he was very, very good at his job. It was also why the idea of the woman getting away with the jewels in Paris on his watch irked.

Broadening the beam of light, he moved toward a collection of snuff boxes. His sources had informed him the boxes were part of the shipment Bliss had received from France just this morning. With any luck, he'd be able to locate the missing merchandise, take the lady jewel thief into custody, then leave town before anyone even knew he'd been here.

After that debacle in Paris, Shayne figured he was due for a change in luck.

AT FIRST MICHAEL O'MALLEY thought it was mice, which didn't make sense, because if there was one thing Bliss Fortune's horrible cat did—other than hiss at him—it was keep the place free of insects and rodents. Michael had proof of the tomcat's industriousness. There'd been more than one morning he'd arrived at work to find a dead mouse lying in front of his door.

Whenever he complained to his landlady, Bliss would merely smile her dazzling, man-melting smile and assure him that the murdered rodent was a gift. Hercules'

way of showing affection. Michael didn't believe that.
Not for a minute.

He held his breath, listening carefully to the sound of
footsteps on the floor below. Having arrived back from
Baton Rouge late, he'd dropped by the office to make
some notes in a file, then, rather than drive home when
he was suffering the effects of a twenty-hour stakeout,
he'd sacked out on his leather couch and had been happily dreaming of a holiday on an island inhabited by
scantily dressed beauties who lived only to please, when
he'd been awakened by the unmistakable sound of foot-
falls.

It could be Bliss, he knew. Perhaps she'd decided
against spending the night in Lafayette. He hoped that
meant she'd been successful at the auction today.

Since his office was located at the top of the stairs, he'd
be able to see the glow of a light through the frosted
glass of his door. The fact that he couldn't was proof that
whoever was down there wasn't The Treasure Trove's
owner.

He stood up, pulled his shoulder holster from the
back of a nearby chair, took out the 9 mm pistol and
made his way gingerly across the floor, intending to con-
front the thief.

As a board squeaked beneath his feet, sounding like a
damn civil defense siren in the hush of the night,
Michael bit back a curse and hoped the sound had been
missed.

It hadn't. Shayne stiffened at the creak above his head.
Every atom in his body went into instantaneous alert,
while he decided whether to fight or flee. Not that there
was any real choice. Shayne had never been the kind of
man to run from a confrontation and although he preferred to think of himself as a lover, not a fighter, when

push came to shove, he was more than willing to do what it took to extricate himself from a sticky situation.

He gingerly pulled his pistol from the back of his belt, went into a crouch, and using both hands to steady his grip, pointed the gun toward the interior door leading to the stairs. The door flew open. An overhead light flashed on, momentarily blinding both men.

There was a moment's stunned shock as the two O'Malley brothers, both holding guns, confronted one another just as they had in those long-ago days when they'd played cops and robbers.

But they were no longer boys. And the guns were not cap pistols, but all too real.

Eyes narrowed, faces grim, they cursed.

Then, Michael and Shayne O'Malley began to laugh at the absurdity of their situation.

BLISS WAS IN a filthy mood. Although she should have spent the day unpacking the shipment from Paris, she'd taken another day away from the office and driven all the way to Lafayette for an antique auction. Unfortunately, she'd been outbid on nearly every item by her old nemesis, Nigel Churchill, who, despite his name and fake British accent, was every bit as American as she was.

"The only reason he bid on that bachelor's chest was because he knew I wanted it," Bliss fumed as she drove back to New Orleans. She was exhausted from the roller-coaster emotionalism of the day. "There's no way he's going to be able to recoup his investment."

Churchill owned a string of antique shops across the South, from Savannah to New Orleans. The women of the Gulf States all seemed to find him incredibly charming, although personally Bliss found his charm less than sincere.

"It's the kind that washes off in the shower," she muttered. "It's slick and slimy. Like skunk oil."

The man seemed determined to corner the entire Southern antiques market. If he couldn't talk a shop owner into selling to him, he'd try less honorable tactics. Bliss had discovered exactly how dishonorable Churchill could be when he'd actually tried to seduce her after she'd turned down his last offer.

After she'd let him know, with no mincing of words, that she'd rather go to bed with an alligator, he'd obviously decided to do whatever he could to keep her from acquiring merchandise. Even if it meant overbidding at every auction they attended.

"I'd rather dump every last saltcellar into the Mississippi River than let that horrid man get his clutches on The Treasure Trove." Her fingers ached; realizing her anger had made her grip the steering wheel too tightly, she flexed them, one hand at a time.

He reminded her a great deal of Alan, who, she recalled grimly, had been the one to introduce her to Churchill in the first place when they'd run into each other during carnival in Venice.

"That's probably why he thought he could seduce me into giving him the store," she muttered. After all, she'd already proven herself susceptible to the appeal of one professional charmer.

"Of course I was younger then."

Only two years, an argumentative little voice in the back of her mind piped up.

"That's a big difference. I was much more naive." Bliss sighed. Unfortunately, she may have gotten older, but it seemed she wasn't that much wiser. At a recent auction Churchill had repeatedly outdid a friend of hers who owned a shop in Houma, which she'd refused to sell to Churchill. She should have suspected he'd use the same tactic again and been ready with a countermove.

Well, that was water under the bridge.

"You still have all that wonderful merchandise from the Paris trip," she reminded herself, choosing to look on the bright side as she enjoyed the sight of the wide white moon floating just in front of the windshield.

That would keep her open for long enough to come up with a new plan to thwart Nigel Churchill's takeover attempts.

"WHAT THE HELL are you doing here?" Michael and Shayne both asked at the same time.

"I rent an office upstairs," Michael said. "Which gives me every legal right to be here."

Shayne conveniently ignored the little dig at his own illegal status. "Bliss Fortune is your landlady?" How, he wondered, had the New Orleans team of investigators missed that all-important fact?

"That's right." Mike folded his arms and glared at the youngest O'Malley brother. "And she's a terrific woman. Which makes me wonder why my spook brother would feel the need to be breaking and entering her shop in the middle of the night."

"It's not exactly the middle of the night," Shayne argued.

Michael cursed. "Lord, I'd forgotten how you never give a straight answer. It's a wonder Mom's hair didn't turn snow white trying to deal with you."

"Roarke and I probably gave her a few gray hairs," Shayne allowed. "But don't forget, she had a secret weapon."

"Such as?"

"You. One false move and we found ourselves answering to our big brother."

"Someone had to keep the two of you in line."

Especially since Dad was never around. Neither brother said it, but Shayne knew they were both thinking it.

"Have you heard from him?"

Michael's glower could have cut granite. "Not since Mom had that surgery a couple years ago. Apparently Roarke told him about it, and he drifted back into town long enough to visit her in the hospital."

"That was big of him."

"Yeah, wasn't it?" Mike's acid expression suggested otherwise.

Their father, Patrick O'Malley, had spent his life roving the world, taking his award-winning news photographs. Although their mother had done her best to raise her three sons, the mantle of masculine responsibility had fallen on Michael's shoulders. Not that he'd ever complained. Indeed, he'd willingly taken on the role of disciplinarian while they'd all been growing up.

He'd even, Shayne remembered now, turned down a baseball scholarship to UCLA, which had cost him a coveted shot at the pros and a longtime girlfriend who'd gone west to school and made new friends, and a new life, without him.

Perhaps because he'd only met his famous father three times in his entire life, Shayne felt only ambivalence toward him. Unlike Mike, who Shayne knew hated Patrick O'Malley for having essentially deserted the family.

"You still haven't answered my question," Michael persisted. "What the hell are you doing here, anyway?"

"I don't suppose you'd believe I was shopping for Mom's birthday present?"

"Her birthday's still two months away."

"She's hard to shop for. I thought I'd get a head start."

"Good try, but I'm not buying it." Mike folded his arms over the front of his white T-shirt. "Want to try again?"

"Geez, you remind me of the time I was sixteen years old and you caught me sneaking into the house five minutes past curfew."

"It was two hours past curfew and you had beer on your breath."

"It's New Orleans," Shayne returned. "Kids don't exactly head straight to the newest soda parlor on Saturday nights." His brother had beat the holy hell out of him for driving drunk, he remembered all too vividly. "I never thanked you." At Mike's arched brow, he added, "For not telling Mom."

Mike shrugged. "She had enough troubles without worrying about her baby boy."

Given his upbringing, Shayne decided it was no wonder Michael had become a cop. That way he could be big brother to the entire damn city. Or at least he had, until he'd gotten caught up in the tangled web of political interests.

"I ran into Roarke in Barcelona. He told me about your problems at the cop shop last year."

Another shrug. "At the time it was hard, bucking the system. You get used to dealing with politicians if you're a cop, especially in this town, but when the powers that be decided it'd hurt tourism if news of a serial rapist running around loose in the Quarter got out before Mardi Gras, I decided I'd had enough.

"But it all worked out for the best because I enjoy

working for myself these days. I take the jobs I want, and turn down the ones I don't...and you still haven't answered my question."

Shayne cursed good-naturedly. "You're just not going to give up, are you?"

"That's not my way."

No, it wasn't. Although all three O'Malley brothers could be accused of being stubborn, Shayne had always thought Mike was undoubtedly the most tenacious. And, unfortunately, the most honorable. Which made this situation even stickier than most.

"I don't suppose you'd believe me if I told you that it's a matter of national security."

"I might believe it," Michael allowed, "but I wouldn't accept it. We're brothers, Shayne. And since I almost blew your head off, I figure that entitles me to some answers. Even if they're supposed to be classified."

"What makes you think you would have ended up getting off the first shot? I'll have you know I passed my last marksmanship test with flying colors."

"Remembering how you always enjoyed getting all those shiny gold stars on your papers back in school, I'm willing to believe you do just fine shooting at paper cutouts of bad guys. But the difference between you and me, baby brother, is that I've actually shot bad guys. While you, on the other hand, have spent your life talking your way in and out of trouble."

It was, of course, all too true. "Anyone ever tell you that your tendency to be right is damn annoying?"

"All the time. But it's one of those little crosses a guy has to bear." Michael's grin faded; his expression became deadly serious again. "Is Bliss in trouble?"

Shayne forced himself to meet his brother's eyes. "Maybe."

"Hell, is it that rat of an ex-husband? The guy's a weasel, Shayne. Not only was he unfaithful, he's no more a polo-playing, Grand Prix-driving jet-setter than you are. The guy was born Bernard Thompson in Minneapolis and ever since he got expelled from Northwestern for selling stolen exams, he's been living by conning women into bed and out of their trust funds."

"I wasn't aware Bliss Fortune even had a trust fund."

"She doesn't. At least not anymore. The weasel managed to fritter away what little savings she did have before she kicked him out."

"Sounds as if you know a lot about her."

"She tried to hire me to get her grandmother's money back after Fortune raided her mutual funds."

"Tried? Are you saying you refused to take the case?"

"I refused any payment," Michael corrected. "After all, it wasn't all that difficult. After I had a little talk with the guy, he saw the light and wrote the old lady a cashier's check for the money he'd embezzled."

"Why do I get the impression that you did a bit more than talk?"

Michael's grin told its own story. "Can I help it if the creep slipped and broke his jaw?"

It was obvious that his brother liked Bliss a lot. And since Shayne had always trusted Mike's instincts about people, he wondered if the Company could be wrong about Bliss Fortune. But then again, he reminded himself, there was a helluva lot of evidence piling up against her. Including that little matter of the phony jewels disappearing from the party she'd attended in Paris.

Of course, her husband had been there, as well. Perhaps, despite the little matter of his alleged infidelity, the two of them were working together. Greed, Shayne knew, was a powerful, age-old motive.

"Does Fortune ever come around?" he asked.

"Are you kidding? Bliss would probably throw one of those antique battle-axes at his head if he tried to stick it in the door."

"That's not the impression I got when I saw them together in Paris."

Michael's eyes narrowed once more to cold blue slits. "There's no way in hell she'd allow herself to become emotionally involved with the bastard again. Which can only mean one thing...are you implying that she's tangled up with the guy in some sort of scam?"

"I'm not implying anything."

"Believe me, if the weasel's implicated her in any way, it's only because he's trying to keep his own tail out of the wringer."

"Despite Fortune's admittedly spotty reputation, I don't think he's involved in this." Other than the fact that he'd shown up unexpectedly at the party, there was nothing to link Bliss's former spouse to the jewel thefts.

"Then what—"

"You gotta keep this one under your hat, Mike."

This time Michael's curse was ripe and hot. "You know, Roarke recently said the same thing to me when he got himself into a jam. At the time, I was tempted to punch out his lights. The same way I'm tempted to remind you that no matter how old you get, I'll always be the older brother. And the stronger one."

That remark triggered old knee-jerk competitive instincts. "Bigger, perhaps," Shayne acknowledged. "But that doesn't mean you could still whup me. I'll have you know, I have a black belt in karate."

"I'm quaking in my boots." The broad grin took the sting of sarcasm from Michael's words.

"Go ahead, sneer all you want. But one of these days,

brother mine, I'm going to knock you down a peg or two."

"You're welcome to try. I haven't had a good knock-down-drag-out fight since I left the force. Probably be healthy to get rid of some aggression by punching that pretty face."

"At least my face doesn't look like ten miles of bad bayou road," Shayne countered. In truth, all three O'Malley brothers looked a great deal alike, although Mike's features were definitely the most harshly drawn.

Mike hit him—not lightly—on the shoulder in a gesture of fraternal fondness. "I'd almost forgotten how much I'd missed you, kid. Welcome home."

"It's good to be back," Shayne said, avoiding the *H* word. He hadn't lived in one place more than six months since he'd graduated from college nearly a decade ago. He wasn't certain that any place would really feel like home.

"You know, it's starting to feel a lot like the old days around here. Roarke's back."

"So I heard. I also heard rumors he'd quit the network."

"He's writing a book. About his adventures as a globe-trotting war correspondent."

Shayne had heard that, as well. "It'll probably sell like hotcakes," he decided. "Especially if the publisher sends him on the road for book signings. I can definitely envision hordes of gorgeous women standing in line to get themselves seduced by the famous O'Malley brother."

"They may get to meet him. But that's all. He's given up bed hopping."

"What?" This was definitely news. Both of his older brothers had taught Shayne many things during his early years. Mike had taught him about honor and re-

sponsibility while Roarke'd passed on a great deal of
what he knew about the opposite sex. The rest Shayne
had picked up on his own, using Roarke's guidelines as
a starting point. "Don't tell me he's joined the priest-
hood like Uncle Gabriel?"

"Roarke a priest?" Mike's deep laugh reverberated
around the cluttered room. "That'd be the day. I didn't
say he'd taken a vow of celibacy," he reminded Shayne.
"He's just monogamous these days."

Shayne felt a vast sense of relief. "That'll never last."

"I wouldn't bet the farm on that one. I think he's serious this time. Of course Daria Shea's special. In that respect she's a great deal like Bliss."

Michael's eyes narrowed and hardened with renewed
warning. "Which brings us back to the original subject.
What the hell are you doing here?"

As he attempted to face down his big brother's scru-
tiny, Shayne realized exactly how Mike had garnered a
NOPD record for confessions. It was not easy escaping
that steady, all-seeing gaze. There was also the little matter of his being like a pit bull gnawing on a particularly
juicy bone. Once he got his teeth into you, he just didn't
let go.

Shayne jumped as something brushed against his
legs. "What the hell?"

"It's just Hercules," Michael muttered, glaring down
at the huge ball of orange fur. "Bliss Fortune's single
flaw."

The cat was weaving its way in figure eights between
Shayne's legs. "I remember you liked animals."

"Most animals. This one's the devil reincarnate."

"Don't you think that's a bit of an exaggeration?"
When Shayne absently leaned down to stroke the bright

fur, the cat arched its back, hissed, and a paw swiped at Shayne's hand, deadly sharp nails fully extended.

Shayne tried to pull away, but proved too slow. "Damn!"

"I warned you," Michael said as they both watched the thin red line appear across the back of Shayne's hand. "And now that I've been proven right yet again, how about telling me what you're doing here?"

Shayne's skin was stinging as if it had been attacked by fire ants. Apparently satisfied, the cat strolled away with feline arrogance, jumped up onto a Queen Anne settee and began washing its huge paws.

The glare Shayne directed its way was a copy of his brother's earlier one. "It's a long story."

"That's convenient. Since I'm not going anywhere, why don't you come upstairs to my office, I'll pour us both a drink and—"

Before he could finish his sentence, there was a rattling of keys in the front door look. A second later they were no longer alone.

"Shayne?" Bliss stared in confusion and disbelief at the man she'd never expected to see again. "What on earth are you doing here in New Orleans? And how did you get in?"

She was looking at him as if she'd just caught him plundering her merchandise. As his mind whirled to come up with a halfway believable answer, the part of him who'd been hoping that he'd exaggerated her appearance these past ten days realized that she was even more appealing than he'd remembered.

Her curly cap of hair flashed like fire and her complexion resembled ivory silk. The shadows beneath her eyes suggested she hadn't been sleeping well since their time together in Paris.

Reminding himself that he hadn't come all the way to New Orleans to catalogue this suspect's feminine attributes, he wondered if Bliss's lack of sleep could possibly stem from a guilty conscience.

"You said if I was ever in the vicinity, I should drop in," he said. "So—" he held both arms out from his sides in an innocent, palms up gesture "—here I am."

Although she'd be the first to admit that she'd behaved uncharacteristically that romantic, stolen evening, Bliss was certain that she'd remember if she'd invited this man to "drop in."

"It's way past closing time," she stated.

"I know. I was planning to show up in the morning," Shayne improvised blithely, "but I was sitting in my hotel room, thinking about you, and I decided just to see what your shop looked like. When I saw the light on—"

"The light was on?" Bliss's gaze shifted to Michael.

"I heard something downstairs," Mike mumbled, his inherent aversion to lying obvious to Shayne, who hoped that Bliss didn't notice her tenant's reluctance to get involved in this discussion. "I figured it was Hercules, so I came downstairs—"

"And heard me knocking." Shayne deftly jumped back into the conversation. "And when he heard I was a friend of yours, he was good enough to let me in."

"I don't understand." Her puzzled gaze moved back and forth between the two brothers. "Why would you let Mr. Broussard into the shop in the first place, Michael?"

Mike shot Shayne a sharp look. Broussard? it seemed to question.

"We're old friends," Shayne said.

"Really." Skepticism touched her eyes. "Michael?"

"As unbelievable as it sounds, that's true. Although

I'll admit the last thing I expected tonight was to open the door and see Shayne standing there."

"I can imagine," she murmured, still obviously distracted. She bent down and scooped up the cat who'd uncurled himself from the chair and come over to stand in front of her. "What are you doing here, Michael, by the way?"

When she began stroking the black-and-orange fur, Hercules' resultant purr sounded like a small motor in the nighttime silence of the shop.

"I got back late from a stakeout and after writing up my report, I decided to crash on the couch."

That made sense, Bliss decided. She turned back toward Shayne, trying not to reveal how pleased she was to see him. Or how disconcerted she was by the feeling. "How about you?"

"How about me, what?"

"What are you doing here in New Orleans?"

"Oh, that's easy." He lifted his shoulders in a nonchalant shrug. "I came to see you, of course."

"You came all the way from Paris just to see me?"

"Of course."

"Of course," she murmured, reminding herself yet again that this was additional proof that Shayne Broussard was a rich man, accustomed to following his whims. "Why?"

Ignoring his brother's laserlike stare, Shayne gave her a slow perusal, his gaze rife with masculine approval as it moved from her bright hair down to her feet, clad in high-topped sneakers, then back up to her face again, lingering on that sweet soft mouth he'd been unable to get out of his mind.

"I'd think that should be self-evident."

Bliss was not unaccustomed to having men look at

her. She was, however, not used to being so vividly aware of her own femaleness as she was whenever this man treated her to one of his blatantly appreciative looks.

Belatedly aware of how disheveled she must look after her long hot day, with her lipstick chewed off, and her unruly hair undoubtedly springing off in all directions, she had a horrible feeling she must look exactly like Little Orphan Annie.

"You shouldn't be here." She was proud that her voice remained amazingly steady, considering the circumstances, but it definitely lacked authority.

"Want me to throw him out?" Mike asked easily. He didn't have to look so damn eager, Shayne thought.

"I don't think that should be necessary." She turned back toward Shayne. "I've had a long day and I'm exhausted. I'm certain Mr. Broussard was just leaving."

With Mike seeming to have switched allegiances, it was now two against one. Preferring better odds, Shayne reminded himself that a tactical retreat was not necessarily a surrender.

"How about breakfast?" he asked. "At Brennan's."

"That's horribly touristy."

"Ah, but I'm a tourist, remember?" Shayne said, ignoring Mike's muffled grunt of disbelief.

"I have to work. I've been away from the store too much as it is, lately."

"Lunch, then."

"I'm sorry, but—"

"I'll pick something up. We can eat in your back office, so you can hear if any customers come in."

"How do you know I have a back office?"

Damn. She was quick. Too quick, Shayne realized. He'd have to be more careful in the future.

"Doesn't every shop?" he asked mildly. "How about it, Bliss?" He dropped his voice to its deepest, most appealing register. "What could a little lunch hurt?"

What indeed? she asked herself knowing, as she did so, the answer. The truth was that Bliss had thought about Shayne Broussard a great deal during the past ten days. Too much for comfort.

She'd be poring over her accounts, seeking an answer to her financial problems that she might have overlooked when his outrageously handsome face would suddenly swirl up in front of her eyes on the lettuce green ledger sheets.

She'd thought about him during the day at work, in the evening while Zelda was chattering away, during much of the drive out to Lafayette today. And heaven help her, she'd dreamed every night of that brief kiss, dreams that had only had her waking up wanting more. Much, much more.

"I don't know..." she vacillated.

To Shayne's immense surprise and gratitude, Mike chose that moment to speak up. "I can vouch for Shayne," he said. "He may be uglier than homemade sin, but he's not such a bad guy, Bliss."

"Thanks for the sterling recommendation," Shayne said with good-natured sarcasm.

"Just trying to help you out," Mike drawled. "Poor boy always has been a mite shy," he told Bliss. "I think it comes from his deep-seated feeling of inferiority."

Bliss laughed while Shayne shot his brother another mock glare. "Since you've come all this way, I suppose the least I can do is have lunch with you."

"Terrific." Shayne rubbed his palms together as if he'd never expected any other outcome. Which, in fact, he hadn't. "I'll be by about one."

"Make it two."

Although he suspected she was simply trying to establish equality right off the bat, Shayne nodded and said, "Two it is." Without giving her time to back away, he lowered his head and brushed a kiss against her forehead. "I'll be counting the minutes."

"Lord, no wonder the poor boy has such bad luck with women," Mike said, laughing. "With lines like that."

"You're just jealous." Shayne's self-satisfied grin widened as he turned toward his brother and held out his hand. "It was nice to see you again, Mike. Perhaps we'll run into each other while I'm in town."

Mike's fingers tightened in a way designed to cause pain, but Shayne refused to flinch. "Count on it."

It could have been a promise. But Shayne knew his brother well enough to know that it was a threat. He may have avoided Michael O'Malley's famed third degree this time, but he hadn't escaped. All he'd succeeded in doing was earning a reprieve. And postponing the inevitable.

He let himself out the door, resisting the impulse to take Bliss in his arms and kiss her properly. There'd be plenty of time for that later.

Shayne had kissed suspects before. Once, a few years ago, he'd even established a relationship of sorts with a former East German spy. Helga had been smart as a whip, a rare natural blonde with a body she'd honed to rock-hard perfection by working out three hours a day.

He'd spent two months feeding her disinformation, knowing she was doing the same thing to him. And the entire time they'd been falling into bed together at every opportunity. Such mixing of work and pleasure hadn't particularly disturbed him. On the contrary, there were occasions when he considered sleeping with the enemy one of the perks of an admittedly deadly business.

Bliss was one of the most enticing women he'd ever met and Shayne had every intention of taking her to bed before his time in New Orleans was over. And then, once he'd satisfied his lust, he'd turn her over to the authorities and move on to the next case. And the next woman.

The plan, and his cover, was perfect, he decided as he strode purposefully back to his hotel. Unfortunately, there was one fly in the ointment. And that was his brother.

Shayne wondered if Mike was romantically involved with his luscious landlady. And then wondered why the idea of the two of them having any sort of emotional relationship bothered him.

As he entered the elegant lobby of the Whitfield Palace Hotel, the winsome clerk behind the desk called out to him.

"You have a message, Mr. Broussard," she said with a flash of white teeth that, along with her artfully tousled cloud of black hair, reminded him of a beauty queen. She handed over the discreet ivory envelope, allowing her fingers to brush his in an unmistakable invitation.

Any other time, he might have been interested. She was, after all, a gorgeous specimen of the female sex. And from the moment he'd checked in earlier that afternoon, she'd let him know that she was definitely available.

Unfortunately, when he compared her to Bliss Fortune, she seemed too artificial. And decidedly too easy. Irritated that he was even bothering to compare this undoubtedly honest, friendly individual with a common jewel thief, Shayne turned his attention to the envelope.

He recognized the precise handwriting immediately. Obviously Cunningham didn't trust him to pull off this job by himself. That idea definitely rankled. As he thanked the desk clerk and took off toward the Blue Bayou Lounge, he failed to see the gray-suited man sitting in a brocade chair behind a gold-veined marble pillar, ostensibly reading today's *Times-Picayune* while surreptitiously observing Shayne's every movement.

4

BONE TIRED, BUT unwillingly intrigued by Shayne Broussard's unexpected arrival in the city, Bliss unlocked the door of the small white carriage house.

"Bliss, darling?" a voice from the parlor called out. "Is that you?"

"If it isn't, you could be in deep trouble," she chided her grandmother. "You shouldn't call out to just anyone who opens the door in the middle of the night, Zelda."

"Oh, fiddlesticks, I've lived nearly eighty years of my life in this town and never worried about things like that."

"Times change." Bliss walked into the room, bent down and kissed her grandmother's cheek. The skin was remarkably unlined, smooth as satin and smelled like Ponds face cream.

"Besides, I knew it was you." Zelda's still-bright blue eyes swept over her only grandchild. "How did things go in Lafayette?"

"Don't ask." Bliss kicked off her shoes and slumped into a wicker chair. "I swear, Churchill seems determined to drive me out of business."

"His granddaddy was meaner than an old alligator. Seems the apple didn't fall far from the tree in this case."

Bliss was accustomed to her grandmother's tendency to mix metaphors. In this case, she decided, both fit. "It appears not." She sighed. "I didn't know you knew Nigel's grandfather."

"He was sweet on me for a time," Zelda revealed.

"I can't imagine any boy in the parish not being sweet on you," Bliss said truthfully. Even now her grandmother was a beautiful woman. The faded sepia photographs from Zelda's younger days showed her to have been stunning.

"I did have my share of beaus." Zelda's eyes softened with long-ago memories. "But I forgot every other man I'd ever flirted with the day I met your granddaddy Dupree."

"At your wedding rehearsal dinner," Bliss prompted. Although she was exhausted, and had heard the story countless times since childhood, she knew she'd never tire of the scandalous tale of her grandparents' passionate meeting.

"Dupree arrived the night before the wedding. He was going to be Nelson's best man and for weeks all I'd been hearing about was his Annapolis roommate, the great and famous Dupree. Dupree did this, Dupree did that, Dupree thought this, said this. Lord, you'd think we were talking about the second coming.

"And then he arrived at the hotel, dressed in his summer whites without a smudge of a wrinkle, looking like some kind of Greek god and I realized that for all his talk, Nelson hadn't been exaggerating. Dupree Lejeune stole my heart the moment I set eyes on him."

"Which caused a problem, since you were supposed to marry his best friend the next morning."

"That was a bit of a dilemma," Zelda conceded. "Especially since although your grandfather was every bit as smitten as me, he did the honorable thing and insisted I marry Nelson as planned."

It was Zelda's turn to sigh. "I was honestly fond of Nelson and do believe we could have had a good marriage, if he hadn't died in that fire on that troop carrier in the Pacific. After all, he was a sweet boy. And I did love him, in a fashion."

"But not like you loved Grandpa."

"No." Zelda's lips curved into a secret smile that hinted at passions Bliss was a bit uncomfortable thinking about her grandmother experiencing. "Every fiber in my body tingled whenever I even thought of Dupree. Which was why I traveled to San Francisco the minute the war in the Pacific ended. Although we'd corresponded after poor Nelson's demise, your grandfather certainly hadn't expected me to be waiting on the dock when his ship came into port."

The smile widened. "I'd already booked a room at the Mark Hopkins Hotel and, taking full advantage of his surprise, I managed to lure the poor man into bed. Afterward, of course, he had no choice but to propose. We were married the following day in Reno."

"I suspect he would have proposed even if you hadn't gone to bed with him."

"Well, of course. But there was no way I was going to allow that magnificent specimen of a man to run around loose with every predatory female in the country out to land herself a husband. The war years had made a lot of women man hungry. And any female with blood flowing in her veins could tell that Dupree Lejeune was offering up a virtual smorgasbord of sensual delights."

Despite the fact that she was a grown woman, and had even been married herself, Bliss felt herself blushing at the idea of her grandmother tangling hotel sheets during a passionate, illicit afternoon with a returning war hero. Even one who resembled a Greek god.

"You were lucky," she murmured. "Finding a man who'd love you to distraction for fifty years."

"Posh. Luck had nothing to do with it darlin'. I did have the good fortune to meet my soul mate. But believe me, if I'd left things up to Dupree, I would have stayed a grieving war widow. I wanted him, Bliss. As dearly as I wanted to breathe. And I would have moved heaven and earth, if necessary, to land him."

"Mama always said polite Southern women didn't chase after men."

"Your mama was a fool. Which was why she ended up pregnant without a husband. And you were an even bigger fool for marrying your scoundrel. Which left you with even more problems than your mama had, and no precious baby to show for it."

"I think it was better I didn't get pregnant when I was married to Alan."

"You may have a point," Zelda conceded. "I hate to think what we would have done if you'd had a little tyke that looked like that low-down, lying skunk." She shook her head, which was still the color of a new penny, thanks to Lady Clairol. "Can you imagine disliking your own child every time you looked at it?"

"I couldn't."

"That's what you say. And knowing your big heart, it could be true. But believe me, baby, I've seen it happen before and it's a pitiful shame for mother and child."

She stood up and walked over to a crystal decanter and poured them both a glass of sherry.

"Shouldn't you be in bed?" Bliss asked, accepting the glass even though her grandmother's favorite wine was too sweet for her own personal tastes.

"When you're my age, darling, you'll discover that you don't like to waste whatever precious time you have left sleeping." Zelda took a long sip of the wine, sighed her satisfaction and topped off her glass before returning to the sofa. "I think it's time we had a little talk."

"Oh?" Bliss's blood turned to ice. Her fingers tightened on the glass. "Is everything all right? I mean, you're not ill or anything?"

"Of course not. I'm fit as a fiddle."

"I seem to recall Dr. Vandergrift's mentioning something about your blood pressure."

"My blood pressure's just fine, thank you. Except when I think about your rat of a former husband, which was what I was doing the last time I had an appointment for my annual physical. Besides, the man's nearly as old as I am. He has no business still practicing medicine," Zelda scoffed.

"He was listed in *Town and Country* magazine as one of the nation's best internists."

"Hah. He probably bought his way onto that list with all the money his ancestors got sacking burned mansions during the war."

Zelda and Dr. Elliot Vandergrift had been arguing for as long as Bliss had been alive. Undoubtedly even longer than that. Personally, she'd always suspected that the physician's interest in her grandmother went beyond the medical.

"If it's not your health, it must be finances," she said glumly, taking a longer sip of her own sherry.

"No. Actually, I've been wondering when you were going to tell me about your trip to Paris."

"I already told you, I found some wonderful things."

"You did tell me that. And since I know how much The Treasure Trove means to you, darling, I'm very pleased for you. But I've been waiting for you to tell me about the man you met there."

"What?" Bliss nearly dropped her glass in surprise. "I don't understand what you're talking about."

"The nuns were right when they wrote on your report cards that it was always obvious when you weren't telling the truth, Bliss. You truly are one pitiful liar. I'm referring to whatever man it is who's had you wandering around with your head in the clouds these past ten days."

"I haven't—"

"Of course you have. And personally, I think it's wonderful. And a delightful change from all the gloom and doom that's been hovering over you like a summer thunderhead the past few months. But since these days I'm forced to live vicariously through the romantic escapades of others, I've been getting a little impatient for you to spill the beans."

Bliss shook her head with dual feelings of frustration and admiration. "Doesn't anything get by you?"

"Not if I can help it. As I said, darlin', I have a lot of time on my hands. That lets me watch people. And think about why they're acting the way they do. You definitely came home from France with something on your mind. And from the faraway look in your eyes, I've suspected you weren't lusting after some fancy painting you saw in the Louvre."

"I met a man," Bliss admitted. "But we didn't spend that much time together."

"Falling in love doesn't necessarily take time."

"It wasn't like you and grandpa. Not really. It was mostly just chemistry."

"Never discount chemistry. It can set a pretty solid foundation for a marriage. Why, despite how much we loved each other, there were more than a few bad patches when chemistry helped keep Dupree's and my marriage going."

"It was just that one night," Bliss continued to argue. "But we didn't do anything," she added quickly as she viewed the knowing look in her grandmother's eye.

"Did I say anything?" Zelda asked innocently.

"No. But you were thinking it."

Zelda didn't deny it. "So, how did you leave things?"

"I told him I wasn't ever going to see him again."

"May I ask why not?"

"Because he's rich."

"Now that's one of the most stupid reasons I've ever heard."

"Alan was rich."

"Alan was pretending to be rich," Zelda reminded her.

"That makes it even worse."

"You may have a point there," Zelda conceded. "However, rich or poor, in truth, the boy was trash."

Since Bliss couldn't argue with that, she didn't say anything.

"What did this man say when you told him you weren't ever going to see him again?"

"I thought, at the time, that he took it quite well."

An auburn-penciled brow lifted. "I do believe I hear a 'but' in that statement."

"All right." Bliss exhaled a long sigh, polished off her too sweet sherry and wished it was something stronger. "I stopped by the shop on the way home and found him waiting there."

"Inside? Lord, child, don't tell me you've gotten yourself mixed up with a cat burglar this time?"

"No. It turns out Michael let him in."

"Aw, the bold Black Irish knight, Michael O'Malley. You know," Zelda said slyly, "a woman could do a lot worse than to marry that man."

It was not the first time her grandmother had suggested such a thing, and Bliss said what she always did. "I like Michael a great deal, as a friend."

"Friends can turn into lovers."

"It'd be too weird. Ever since he leased the office over the shop, he's become like my big brother."

"So you keep saying." Zelda sighed, seeming to give up on a match between her granddaughter and her favorite private detective. "Tell me about this other man. The one who followed you all the way from Paris."

"There's really not much to tell."

As she'd thought back over it the past days, Bliss had belatedly realized that she'd done most of the talking that enchanted night. Which meant that Shayne knew almost everything about her. While she knew next to nothing about him.

"What's his name?"

"Shayne. Shayne Broussard."

"Is he French?"

"American."

"What does he do to make all this money you seem determined to reject?"

"I'm not sure. He seemed like a playboy."

"Oh." Zelda's enthusiasm seemed to wane reluctantly. "Well, I'm sure you'll do the right thing, darling."

Even as Bliss agreed, she couldn't quite overlook the problem that when it came to Shayne Broussard, her heart and her head were not even the slightest bit in agreement.

SOMEONE HAD BROKEN into his room. Shayne sensed the intrusion the moment he entered. He pulled out his pistol.

"There's no need for violence," the familiar voice said.

"Dammit, Cunningham," Shayne ground out as he flicked the light switch. "What the hell are you doing here?"

The older man appeared unperturbed by Shayne's barely restrained temper. "As it happens, I heard a bit of news that I thought you might be interested in."

"You've never heard of the telephone?"

"Phones can be tapped. Even so-called secured lines."

"What makes you think this room isn't bugged?"

"I swept it, of course. As you would have when you first checked in."

Since it was the truth, Shayne didn't bother to argue the point. "So, what's this earth-shattering news that had to be delivered personally?"

Cunningham sipped from the brandy he'd taken from the minibar. Shayne immediately reminded himself to include the overpriced miniature bottle on his expense account reimbursement report. No way was he going to spring for the outrageous cost.

"There are rumors of a contract."

Every atom in Shayne's body leapt to instant alert but practice allowed him to maintain his expressionless stare. "Contracts aren't unusual in our business."

"True." Obviously enjoying drawing out the moment, Cunningham took another drink. "Even ones between husbands and wives. Or, should I say former husbands and ex-wives."

"Alan Fortune took a contract out on his wife?"

That didn't make sense, Shayne thought. From what he'd been able to tell, the guy had gotten out of that marriage like the bandit he'd turned out to be.

"That's one scenario making the rounds." Steel gray eyes looked at him over the rim of the cut crystal glass that was standard in the hotel whose worldwide motto was When Deluxe Will No Longer Do. Since the New Orleans Whitfield Palace was the flagship hotel in the international chain, it was even more luxurious than most. "Another possibility is that Bliss Fortune took the contract out on her husband."

"That's ridiculous." Shayne crossed the room, pulled a beer from the minibar refrigerator and popped the cap.

"Murder for hire is usually about money. The woman is in debt right up to her pretty green eyeballs."

"She wouldn't have it in her to kill anyone."

A pewter brow arched. "You've determined that from a few hours of conversation and a stroll in the moonlight?"

"No. I've determined that from a few hours of conversation, a natural gift for being able to read people, and weeks spent poring over every bit of information about both Fortunes I could uncover. She's the quintessential do-gooder. I doubt if she could step on a cockroach."

"Which is exactly how some people might view Alan Fortune," Cunningham murmured. "Very few con men are murderers. They don't have to kill for profit since they get what they want with charm and guile."

"It doesn't matter," Shayne insisted. "Because unless she's got an insurance policy stashed away somewhere on the guy that no one's uncovered, killing him would probably only result in her having to pay funeral expenses."

"The guy does appear to be a bit dependent on the generosity of women," Cunningham agreed.

"More than a bit. He's already dumped the model for a newly divorced princess who's paying for his gambling vacation in Monaco."

After watching the embrace between husband and wife at the party, Shayne had made it a point to keep track of Fortune's whereabouts. Not because of any personal interest in Bliss, he'd told himself, knowing that was yet another lie. It was bad enough to lie for a living; he figured when a guy began lying to himself, he was on the verge of real trouble.

"My sources tell me that the princess is more than a little generous," Cunningham conceded. His eyes, which were two shades grayer than his steely crew cut, turned thoughtful as he looked into the depths of the amber liquor, as if searching for the answer to some problem that had been vexing him. "That guy must be dynamite in the sack."

Unbidden, an image of Bliss Fortune's long legs wrapped around her ex-husband's naked hips flashed in front of Shayne's mind like a scene from a dirty movie. "What the hell brought that up?"

"He can call himself a venture capitalist all he wants, but the truth is he's nothing but a gigolo who had the good luck to be born with great looks. He reminds me of that actor—what's his name—the one who looks like Redford that all the women are going nuts over these days?"

"Brad Pitt." Again Shayne felt an unpleasant tug of something that felt too damn much like jealousy for comfort. "I assume there's a point to this?"

"The point is, that even if the guy is scum, he's damn good-looking scum. Add to that the fact that he's got a reputation for international bed hopping and I'd say you've got a motive for Bliss Fortune to want him dead."

Shayne couldn't believe this. "This isn't a case of a woman scorned. She kicked him out when she discovered he'd been cheating on her."

"She could have decided he got off too easily, that he deserves more...punishment." Cunningham grinned wickedly. "The nights are long down here in the South.

And hot. She's undoubtedly going to be ripe for a little action, so you shouldn't have any problem keeping close to her. The only thing to worry about is whether you can come up to Fortune's performance."

"Correction. The only thing I'm worried about is whether or not I could get drummed out of the service for planting my fist in the middle of my superior's face."

"I'd say that's a given." Cunningham's voice turned as steely as the rest of him. "We've already got the Fortune woman pegged as a thief and a smuggler. Now that it looks like she's not above murder for hire, I thought I ought to warn you."

"Consider me warned," Shayne snorted through clenched teeth.

"Well, now that I've done my duty, I think I'll wander over to Bourbon Street and take in a few of those nudie shows. I don't suppose you'd feel like coming along?"

"I think I'll pass."

"Your loss. But I guess you'll want to get your beauty sleep. Before your lunch tomorrow with your lady friend." When Shayne's gaze hardened, the older man laughed. "Don't forget, I know everything. Which is why I'd watch my back if I were you. Bliss Fortune may look as sweet as spun sugar, but we both know that looks are definitely deceiving. And although we've had our differences, O'Malley, I sure wouldn't want you to end up like a black widow male on his wedding night."

Point made, he left Shayne to think about this latest news. And although he still believed Bliss was incapable of killing anyone, he also had to admit that revenge was a powerful motive.

What if she'd hired someone to take her husband out?

he wondered. It suddenly occurred to him that she might know more about him than he believed.

What if their meeting hadn't been entirely accidental? What if she'd been setting him up the same time he'd been setting her up? The idea, as improbable as it seemed, was not exactly impossible. After all, the old "Spy Vs Spy" comic strip that had run for years in *Mad* magazine depicted just such a ridiculous scenario.

"What if she wants me to be the triggerman?"

The moment he heard the words come out of his mouth, Shayne laughed. The idea was ludicrous.

"But so is murder for hire in the first place," he reminded himself.

Swearing viciously, he went over to the window, opened the drapes, looked out on the famed City that Care Forgot, and wondered what the hell he'd gotten himself into this time.

FORTUNATELY, THE NEXT morning was busy in The Treasure Trove, which kept Bliss's mind off her scheduled lunch date with Shayne Broussard and her eyes from constantly glancing down at her watch.

A busload of German tourists had arrived at the French Quarter from the Hyatt and were going through their traveler's checks as if they'd just received word that the world was going to end tomorrow and the person left with the most antiques would win.

Wonderfully, unlike so many other customers, they also seemed to find dickering unnecessary. They not only willingly paid the sticker price, but readily agreed to whatever it cost to send their purchases back home.

"Can you believe this?" Lilah Middleton, Bliss's assistant, said as she wrapped up a Sheraton tea caddy painted with foliate swags. Although Bliss had suggested against it, the buyer had insisted on carrying this item home in his luggage. "It's like the invasion of the Luftwaffe."

"It's also going to pay this month's rent," Bliss answered under her breath as she wiped her damp forehead.

Although the shop was air-conditioned, the ancient system was failing to keep up with the constant opening and closing of the door as customers streamed in and out of The Treasure Trove. The temperature outside was nearing ninety; Bliss suspected the crush of bodies was making the indoor temperature nearly as high.

"So we should be grateful." Bliss pulled out some more wrapping paper from beneath the counter, cursing inwardly as a small cannister rolled onto the floor. Thank goodness the pepper spray, which Michael and Zelda had insisted she keep handy, hadn't self-detonated.

"Oh, I'm not complaining," Lilah said. "Actually it's nice to be busy." She glanced around the shop. "Oh, dear."

Bliss followed her gaze to a rotund woman with apple cheeks who was looking into the locked glass case of stuffed animals, checking out a turn-of-the-century Steiff plush teddy bear. "What's wrong?"

"I had a customer in the shop yesterday morning who was considering buying that bear. I promised to hold it for twenty-four hours, but then the phone rang, and I guess I forgot to put a Hold sign on it."

"Yesterday morning?"

"A bit before lunch."

Bliss checked her watch. "Well, since it's after noon, the deadline's up."

"But this was a local," Lilah said. "She mentioned living at Audubon Place."

"Oh." That did, after all, make a big difference. The chances of the German lady ever returning were nil, unlike someone who lived in the gated, privileged environs of Audubon Place, where some of the most luxurious homes in the city were located. "Why don't you finish ringing up this biscuit box and powder case and I'll take care of it."

Bliss took the key for the case that housed the teddies from the cash register drawer, went out from behind the elaborately carved antique counter and approached the woman. "Welcome to The Treasure Trove," she said with her brightest, most professional smile as she unlocked the case and took out the bear. "Do you have an interest in bears?"

"Ya," the woman answered, nodding enthusiastically. She stroked the brown plush fur, her appreciative gaze as bright as the stuffed animal's boot button eyes.

"I'm afraid this one has suffered some wear."

"That's good." The woman smiled. "It shows it was much loved."

Damn. Bliss had used that same argument to push a black bisque-headed baby doll just last week.

"The growler doesn't work," she pointed out.

"No matter."

From the way the woman continued to stroke the bear's soft plush fur, Bliss knew she'd already fallen in love with it. Understanding such sentiment well—which was how she'd gotten into the antique business in the first place—she decided to give it one last shot. Then, if the woman held firm, in the event the Audubon Place customer actually did return, she'd just have to try to finesse her way through the situation.

"Have you seen this one?" she asked, pointing out a cinnamon plush bear with the Steiff tag still in its ear. "It's just a bit newer—it was made in Nuremberg in 1910—but it's in near perfect condition. And see—" she squeezed the hump "—the growler still works."

The low rumble seemed to appeal to the shopper. But her eyes narrowed as she checked the small cardboard price tag. "It is also more expensive."

"Oh dear, that's an oversight," Bliss improvised quickly. "I was out of town yesterday and my assistant undoubtedly didn't have time to mark all the sale items." She glanced over at Lilah who was watching the exchange.

"I'm sorry," Lilah said on cue. "Things got so busy yesterday afternoon, I forgot that bear was one of the special items."

"Special items?" the German woman asked, her interest suddenly piqued.

"Oh, yes," Bliss said. "We'd planned to take two hundred dollars off the price." Which now put it fifty dollars below the bear the woman had been looking at in the first place.

While Bliss held her breath, the woman hesitated, her gaze going from one to the other. But she continued to hold on to the first bear.

"And free shipping." It was Bliss's final offer.

Another long pause settled in.

Finally, the customer returned the original brown bear to its shelf. "I will take this one," she decided, picking up the cinnamon one.

"I think you've made an excellent choice." Bliss hurried over to the counter before the woman could change her mind.

"Now go rescue that other one," she said under her

breath to Lilah, who didn't hesitate to do exactly as told while Bliss took a handful of white tissue paper from beneath the counter and began wrapping it around the bear she'd just sold for the same price she'd paid for it during her recent trip to France.

It was, admittedly, a gamble. But then again, she decided as she chatted cheerfully with the woman and continued to package up the purchase, so was life.

That idea brought to mind her trip to Paris and the serendipitous way she'd met Shayne, and their upcoming lunch. As she had all during the long and mostly sleepless night, Bliss considered calling the hotel and canceling their date.

But after having traveled all this way, she doubted he'd take no for an answer. And, although she hated to admit it, she was looking forward to seeing him again.

5

A STICKLER FOR details and punctuality, Shayne arrived at The Treasure Trove at precisely two o'clock. The bells tied to the door tinkled merrily, but he doubted Bliss could hear them over the din in the store. He hadn't heard so much German since his disinformation days hanging out with Helga in Düsseldorf.

He moved out of the doorway to stand in the shadow of a tall case clock and enjoyed the advantage of watching her undetected.

Her face was flushed from the heat in the small cramped shop, her curls were a wild fiery halo around her head, and she appeared to have chewed off most of her lipstick. But she was still one of the most dazzling creatures he'd ever seen.

Her eyes warmed everyone she spoke with as she rang up a steady stream of purchases. Her smile was quick and genuine, basking the recipient in Southern sunshine. Somehow she managed to answer questions, ring up sales, package purchases and hand out sight-seeing tips without missing a beat.

She was clearly in her element, unlike the party in Paris, where her wood sprite energy had appeared so out of sync with the studied, almost bored nonchalance of the French.

As if sensing his steady silent appraisal, she suddenly looked up, and met his gaze. Although he fought against it, Shayne found the rush of additional color into her already pink cheeks the most charming thing he'd ever witnessed.

She recovered quickly. "Hi," she called out to him. "I hope you don't mind waiting. As you can see, I'm a little tied up at the moment."

"Now that's an intriguing thought." His voice was quiet, the comment spoken more to himself than to her, but since everyone else in the shop had chosen that moment to fall quiet, his words rang out like the chimes of nearby St. Louis Cathedral.

The color edging her high-cut cheekbones deepened, reminding him of the rosy azaleas in his mother's garden.

"You go ahead and take care of business," he answered, fully aware of the appraisal of more than one woman in the room. Including the busty blond clerk who looked as if she belonged in a *Playboy* pictorial featuring Belles of the Bayou States. "I'll just look around."

"We can always reschedule."

He laughed at that. "Good try. But I'm a patient man."

That said, he turned his attention to a leather-bound book of old maps that had been on the manifest of the items shipped from Paris. There was no way she could have managed to hide the jewels between these thin parchment pages. He'd just have to keep looking.

Nearby, Hercules was lying atop a needlepoint pillow in a pool of sunshine. When Shayne glared at him, the cat haughtily turned his head away and began washing his paws.

"Who in heaven's name is that gorgeous man?" Lilah hissed as the two women continued to ring up sale after sale.

"Just a man."

"Honey, far be it from me to argue with the boss, but you're dead wrong.... Here you go," she said, handing over the safely packaged frosted-glass perfume bottle to a dour fifty-something German. "Enjoy."

The woman responded with a grunt.

"Cheerful, isn't she?" Lilah muttered.

"She may not speak English," Bliss replied, grateful for the change in subject.

But Lilah was not to be deterred. "Tom Selleck is just a man," she said. "Brad Pitt, Val Kilmer, Keanu Reeves, George Clooney are all just men. But that guy—" she glanced over at Shayne who'd moved on to a collection of Confederate army swords and sighed deeply "—is a divine being."

"I suppose he's good-looking enough, if you're interested in that type," Bliss allowed.

"Tall, dark, built and handsome? Who isn't?"

"Me." Bliss only wished her tone held more conviction.

"If that's the case, hon, then I think I'd better call the men from the funny farm to come take you away in one of those nice comfy straitjackets." Lilah stopped in the act of tearing tape off the dispenser and gave Bliss a long, probing look. "Oh, hell. He's rich, isn't he?"

"Filthy."

"Now that is truly a crime." Lilah shook her head. "Honestly, Bliss, don't you think it's time you stopped tarring an entire class of men with that brush your rat of a husband left you holding?"

It was the same thing Lilah had been telling her for months. The same thing Zelda had told her. The same thing Shayne had suggested their night together in Paris.

Lilah pressed her case. "You're the one always saying people shouldn't be prejudiced."

"Point made." Bliss forced a smile as she greeted a stocky man who'd come up to the register gingerly carrying an old Raggedy Ann doll. "Oh, that's one of my favorites."

"For my daughter," he said.

"I'm sure she'll love it. I certainly did." Bliss did not add that there'd been a time when she'd hoped to save the well-worn rag doll for her own daughter to play with some day.

He arched a blond brow. "This was your doll?"

"It was a very long time ago." *Terrific. Open mouth, ruin sale*, Bliss thought. "As you can see, I've grown up and moved beyond dolls. But I'm sure your daughter will be thrilled."

"I hope so." He frowned. "She is very young. But it seems girls grow up much faster in Germany these days."

"In America, too." Bliss experienced a fleeting sense of loss as she folded the doll's floppy arms and legs into a box. Business was business, she reminded herself firmly. If she hadn't wanted to sell the damn doll, she shouldn't have brought it down to the store.

He paid for the doll, took the package and left the store. Busy ringing up a trio of inkwells, Bliss didn't notice Shayne leave the shop.

It was nearly three o'clock when the store finally emptied. Glancing around for the first time in an hour, Bliss realized she and Lilah were totally alone. Obviously, Shayne's patience had reached its limits. She told herself she should feel good about this, but Bliss was vaguely disappointed that he hadn't waited.

"My feet are killing me," Lilah complained, sagging down onto the rush seat of a painted pine chair.

"You shouldn't wear heels to work."

"True." She kicked off the strappy high-heeled sandals and wiggled her toes. "But I have a dinner date tonight and wasn't going to have time to change, and it's been so slow around here lately, I thought I could get away with it. Hell, how was I to know that we were going to get overrun by a horde of huns?"

She groaned at the sound of the bells signaling another customer, then flashed her teeth in the same smile that had gotten her named Mardi Gras Queen her senior year at LSU.

"Well, hello." Her drawl was as rich as pralines. "I was afraid you'd left Bliss in the lurch."

"Never happen." Shayne's answering grin was unreasonably cocky. Even as she warned herself of its dangers, Bliss found herself attracted. "I just decided to get out of the way until the crowd dispersed." He turned toward Bliss. "You look wiped out."

"Flatterer," she muttered, pushing a damp, wayward curl out of her eye.

When the rebellious curl immediately bounced back, Shayne crossed the room and plucked a small, mother-of-pearl comb from a satin-backed display beside the cash register.

"Here. Let me help." His fingers brushed against her too warm temple as he pushed the curl back and secured it with the comb. "There. Perfect."

Bliss didn't know which she hated more. The way his touch caused her pulse to leap or his unwavering confidence. A rich man's confidence, she reminded herself.

"That just happens to be shop merchandise."

"Not anymore." He reached into his pocket, took out a gold clip, peeled a few bills off the top and laid them on the counter. "Because I just bought it."

"Then you should keep it," Bliss countered with

feigned sweetness as she plucked the comb from her hair, damning the rebellious curl.

There was a battle of wits going on, Shayne realized as he looked at the delicate shell-like comb in her palm, then up at the determination glittering in her eyes. "As nice as it is, it's not really my style."

"Surely you have a woman friend you can give it to."

"I just did."

"Oh, for heaven's sake, Bliss," Lilah complained, rising to her feet with a lazy feline grace Bliss had envied on more than one occasion. The kind designed to capture and hold a man's attention. "Would you quit being such a stick-in-the-mud and take the damn comb?"

Taking matters into her own hands, she plucked the comb in question from Bliss's hand and stuck it back in place. "There. That looks absolutely lovely." She smiled at Shayne again. "You have excellent taste."

He smiled back, but didn't take his gaze from Bliss's face. "I know."

A silence settled over them, as deep and dark and steamy as the bayou at midnight.

"Gracious." Lilah picked up a satin, lace-trimmed fan from the counter and began fluttering it dramatically. "Is it getting hotter in here, or is it just me?"

"That's it." Bliss snapped out of the trancelike state Shayne's presence seemed to have induced, snatched her purse from beneath the counter and glared up at the object of all her consternation. "Did you say something about lunch?"

"Absolutely." He turned toward Lilah. "Can you lock up?"

"Of course."

He flashed another of those woman-killing smiles

Bliss was beginning to hate. "Terrific." He cupped her elbow. "I don't know about you, but I'm starved."

"Wait just a minute." Bliss dug in her heels as he tried to urge her out of the store. "I'm not staying away until closing."

"That's what you think. You agreed to lunch, remember?"

"Yes, but—"

"And what I have in mind will take awhile."

"There are any number of wonderful places right here on the block. After all, New Orleans is known for its food," she insisted. "Why, just off the top of my head, I could probably name a dozen—"

"Bliss." He touched a fingertip to her lips. "You're beginning to babble again, sweetheart. The same way you did in Paris."

"Paris?" Lilah snapped to immediate attention. "You two were in Paris together?"

"We met at a party," Shayne said. "Didn't Bliss tell you?"

"No." Lilah folded her arms across the front of her short, tight dress. "Other than the fact that she found lots of needed stock, the only other thing she mentioned about the trip was that she'd blasted through all her credit card limits."

Shayne slowly shook his head as he looked down at Bliss. "I'm crushed."

"Somehow I doubt that," she muttered, knowing she was going to face intense questioning from her longtime friend.

It was bad enough being interrogated by Zelda. Beneath Lilah's soft cotton-candy-pink exterior dwelt the original steel magnolia. The woman could be downright ruthless when it came to extracting personal secrets.

"It was, without a doubt, one of the most romantic nights of my life," he informed Lilah, whose eyes widened further at this little newsflash. "Strolling along the Left Bank at midnight, sharing pastries in a little out-of-the-way bistro, the violin player..." He looked back down at Bliss. "I still have that chalk drawing the artist did. I look at it several times a day and think about you. Which is why I realized I had no choice but to track you down."

"Be still my heart." Lilah sighed dramatically and patted her breast. "If you don't want this guy, Bliss, the least you should do is give the rest of us a shot." She fluttered her lashes in her best Southern belle manner. "How do you feel about blondes?"

"They're my favorite. Right after mouthy redheads," he added.

"This is getting more ridiculous by the minute," Bliss huffed. "All right, if it'll shut you up, I'll go to lunch wherever you want. Lilah, please close up the shop. And, if you don't mind, would you feed Hercules?"

"Like the beast would starve if he missed a meal," Shayne muttered.

"Do you have something against cats, Mr. Broussard?"

"Only monster ones who decide to take my hand off." He held out the hand in question.

Viewing the angry red slash mark, Bliss decided against admitting that she was the only person who could get along with the huge stray she'd rescued back when he'd been a kitten caught outside her store during a monstrous summer thunderstorm.

"I should probably give him an extra helping of kibbles for being such a good guard cat," she said mildly before turning back to an openly amused Lilah. "Oh, and if Michael shows up before you leave, would you please tell him that if I don't come back to finish this month's books tonight he's to send out the Saint Bernards. And the storm troopers."

"Whatever you say, boss." Lilah returned a languid salute. "However, ending the evening working on ledger sheets sounds like a horrendous waste. If it were me..."

"It's not," Bliss snapped uncharacteristically.

"Low blood sugar," Shayne suggested smoothly. "It's obviously made her cranky." This time he put his hand possessively on her hip. "Come along, darlin', let's get you something to eat before you swoon."

Frustrated as she was, Bliss didn't notice the way his deep voice had unconsciously slid into the soft sound of his Louisiana roots. "I've never swooned in my life."

"Good for you. But there's always a first time for everything.... Goodbye, Miz—" he paused, "I just realized I didn't catch your name." He knew, of course, exactly who the blonde was. But there wasn't any way to admit that. He'd almost made a stupid, careless mistake, which wasn't at all like him.

"That's probably because I didn't toss it," Lilah suggested silkily. "It's Lilah. Lilah Middleton."

"It's a pleasure to meet you, Lilah," Shayne answered with the politeness drilled into him by his Southern mother. "I'm Shayne Broussard."

"Believe me, the pleasure is all mine." Lilah dimpled prettily and fluttered her lashes. "And if Bliss decides to throw you back into the dating pool, I'm in the book."

Shayne had been away for so long he'd forgotten exactly how forward Southern women could be. They had learned, he recalled now, the trick of coating their lack of reserve in sugared flirtaciousness so that they never appeared as aggressive as Yankee females.

"I'll definitely keep that in mind," he promised.

Actually, now that she'd brought it up, if he struck out with Bliss, Shayne thought, getting close to her assistant would probably be the next best thing. And Lilah Middleton had already made it clear that he wouldn't need to put in for hardship pay.

"You do that, darlin'." She waggled her pink-tipped fingers. "You two have fun, now."

"You really are impossible, you know," Bliss said as they walked down Pirate's Alley toward where he'd parked his car across the street from Jackson Square.

"You're not the first person to suggest that," Shayne said mildly.

"And I doubt if I'll be the last."

"Probably not."

"You don't have to be so damn agreeable," she muttered, wanting to dislike him, but finding it more and more difficult. "Especially since I know you're a fraud."

"Oh?" He stopped and looked down at her, his face as smooth as newly polished glass.

Sensing something new, something different, Bliss glanced up at him in surprise. And although she wasn't positive, because it came and went so quickly, she thought she detected a flash of ice in his eyes.

"It's easy for rich people to be agreeable," she explained. "Since they get everything they want."

"Is that what you really think? That I get everything I want?"

"Don't you?"

He laughed at that, but the sound held scant humor. "Hardly."

Shayne Broussard irritated her, frustrated her, and

dammit, interested her. "So, what do you want that you haven't been able to get?"

He began walking again. "Well, there's you to start with."

"You're going to have to manage to survive without that one," she said dryly. "What else?" She was, Bliss realized as they crossed Decatur Street, suddenly curious.

"That's the hell of it," Shayne confessed. "I don't know."

For the second time in as many minutes, he'd let the mask he'd worn for nearly a decade drop just long enough to give Bliss a glimpse of the real man hiding beneath the pleasant, urbane exterior. There *was* something there moments ago, she decided. Something that was dark, ice-cold and and potentially dangerous. And just now she'd sensed a certain sadness.

Telling herself she was being fanciful, that her imagination was running wild after a sleepless night and a busy day, she shook off the strange feeling.

"When you figure it out, let me know."

"You'll be the first I tell."

The funny thing was, as he stopped beside a sleek Jaguar convertible, she decided he wasn't kidding.

"Nice car," she murmured.

He opened the passenger door with the flair of a man born and bred in the South. "I can take it back to the rental place and see if they have an old battered Pinto or Pacer."

Her lips curved into a reluctant smile as she slid into the buttery soft seat redolent of sun-warmed leather. "Don't you dare."

She waited until he was backing out of the parking lot beside the old Jackson Brewery building, then sighed and said, "At least you can't accuse me of not being well-balanced."

He glanced over at her as he paused for a clutch of tourists, laden with shopping bags, crossing the street. "I'm afraid that reference escapes me."

Bliss was woman enough to admit when she was behaving abominably. "I suppose, if pressured, I'd have to admit that the past couple years, I seem to have acquired a chip on both my shoulders."

He threw back his head and laughed at that, a rich bold laugh that cleared the air and sent streamers of warmth flowing through her.

"I knew there was a reason I liked you. Besides your wraparound legs and drop-dead gorgeous face."

Not knowing how to answer that without getting herself into hot water, Bliss didn't respond.

Shayne drove another two blocks before he glanced over at her and said, "Now it's your turn."

"My turn?"

"To say something nice about me."

"Oh." She pretended to give the matter grave consideration. "I already told you. This is a nice car."

"That would only be a compliment if I'd designed and built it. Want to try again?"

She thought again. "I suppose you're not bad looking. Actually, now that I think about it, you remind me a lot of Michael."

"Mike?" He'd been wondering if she'd caught the resemblance to his older brother. "Really?"

She gave him a long, judicial look. "His features are more harshly drawn, but yes, there's definitely a resemblance. You look a lot like his brother, Roarke, too."

"So you know Roarke?"

"We've met. He's currently living with an assistant

district attorney. They've bought a few pieces of furniture for their house."

Roarke antique shopping. Now that was a revelation, Shayne decided. He also vowed to wrap this case up as soon as possible, if for no other reason than to meet the wonder woman who'd managed such a miracle.

"So," he said with studied nonchalance, "do you and Mike have a thing going?"

She was about to point out that her relationship with Michael O'Malley really wasn't any of this man's business, then reluctantly admitted that wasn't exactly true. Because although she was uncomfortable admitting it, even to herself, something was happening between her and Shayne.

"We're just good friends."

Shayne didn't like the cool feeling of relief triggered by her words. She was just an assignment, he reminded himself. It would be a mistake to forget that.

Bliss settled back in the glove-soft leather bucket seat, enjoyed the feel of the warm soft air on her face and watched the scenery that was both familiar and beloved flash by.

"Where are we going?"

"I don't suppose you'd just trust me to surprise you?"

Bliss remembered a time when trust had come easily to her. But that was before Alan. "I think I'd like some idea."

"Okay. I thought, perhaps, we could have a picnic."

"A picnic?"

"Bad idea?"

"Actually, it's a wonderful idea," she admitted. "It's just that I thought you'd prefer something else."

"Some overpriced restaurant where the waiters snub

you in phony French accents while handing you a pretentious twelve-page wine list?"

"Something like that." She sighed. "I'm sorry. My prejudices are showing again, aren't they?"

"It seems to be a knee-jerk response," Shayne said mildly. "I suppose there's a story behind it?"

"Not one I want to talk about. Not today." Her tone, and her gaze, as she turned toward him, were firm.

Shayne shrugged. "Whatever you say. We've got lots of time to get to know one another."

"Oh?" Against her will, her curiosity was piqued. "How long are you planning to stay in town?"

"It all depends."

"On what?"

"How my business turns out."

"Oh."

She couldn't keep the disappointment that she wasn't the real reason for his trip to New Orleans from her voice. Which was ridiculous, Bliss reminded herself firmly. She certainly hadn't wanted him to come here in the first place.

Her second thought was to wonder when she'd become such a liar.

6

IF SHE'D BEEN SURPRISED by Shayne showing up at her shop, his next words stunned her.

"I've recently bought a home in the city," he said off-handedly. "And as it happens, I need someone to help me furnish it."

"I don't believe this."

"What?"

"Do you actually believe you can buy your way into my bed?"

"Your bed?" He paused at a red light at the corner where tourists were boarding a green streetcar. "Surely you don't think a handsome, wealthy, witty man such as myself needs to hand out money to get women to go to bed with him?"

No. She had no doubt that he had any number of gorgeous women on at least two continents vying for that opportunity.

"If that's not the reason, then I suppose this is where I inform you that I don't take charity. From anyone."

"I'm not offering charity, dammit," he said through clenched teeth.

This wasn't going at all the way he'd planned. What he'd planned was a lazy sun-filled afternoon, when he'd ply the lady with some rich food, a little wine, lower her defenses with a few kisses perhaps, then ease his way around the barricades she'd erected around herself. Instead, he went blurting out his plans like a pimply-faced sixteen-year-old asking the school beauty queen to the Junior Prom.

"I was suggesting a business arrangement. Nothing more. Nothing less. I have a house that's in need of furniture. Since it's from the antebellum period, it only makes sense that they should be either genuine antiques or very good reproduction pieces. However, since I can't tell the difference, I need an expert and having checked you out—"

"You checked me out?"

"Of course. And everyone I've spoken with sings your praises. So, it only made sense that I ask you to take on the job."

The light changed, allowing him to cross the neutral zone into the American sector of the city. "And believe me, sweetheart, if and when I decide to take you to bed, you'll know. Because I'm a straight-shooting sort of guy."

It was the most outrageous lie he'd told her. But it was important that she believe him. Important for him, and, if she was mixed up with the group of deadly individuals Cunningham and his superiors believed she was, important for her as well. She might be a thief, but she'd be a great deal more useful to him alive than dead.

Shayne's voice, which had always been warm and edged with a certain undeniably appealing humor, had turned as granite hard as his face. As they passed the Victorian Gothic Trinity Episcopal Church, Bliss decided that Shayne Broussard was not quite the easy-going jet-set playboy she'd first taken him for.

"When, exactly, were you planning to show me this alleged house?" She still couldn't believe what he was suggesting.

"Right now. I thought we could eat lunch there."

"Alone?"

"Afraid to be alone in an empty house with me, Bliss?"

"No," she answered, not quite honestly.

"You probably should be," he admitted. "Mike would undoubtedly warn you that I could be a pervert rapist or killer."

She remembered thinking that very same thing when she'd gone off with Shayne in Paris. "Are you?"

"Of course not. However, if I were, I'd hardly tell you."

"Good point."

"Actually, I figured you'd have a better sense of what I wanted in the house, if we could spend some time in it. That way, you'll know what you're getting into if you decide to accept the job."

"I suppose that makes sense," she agreed. "But why did you buy a house in the first place?"

"Since my company deals in gas and oil leases, I've been meaning to establish a base office in Louisiana for a long time. Then I met you, and coincidentally, a few days later the real estate broker I was working with sent me the brochure for the house, which had just come on the market, and it seemed like fate."

"Is it large?" Since they were currently in the Garden District, Bliss suspected it was a long way from the carriage house she and Zelda shared.

"Enormous. It's one of those mansions that cotton built. It'll be one helluva job if you decide to take it on."

Part of him felt vaguely guilty for conning her this way. Another part remembered those paste jewels that had disappeared the night of the party.

Bliss couldn't deny the excitement that was sparking

like electricity through her veins. Such a commission would be marvelous challenge. Not to mention being highly lucrative. She could undoubtedly pay off all her bills and run the store for a year on the profits.

"Why me?"

"I told you, you come highly recommended. And besides, when I first saw you in Paris, I could tell that you were a woman of rare and special tastes."

"I thought the first thing you noticed about me was my wraparound legs."

"True. Your business skills were a bit down on the list, somewhere below your silk fire hair. But believe me, Bliss, I noticed them."

Since it had been a very long time since she'd felt good about anything, Bliss allowed herself to bask in the glow of that compliment for a moment, then felt obliged to comment on his plans for his new home.

"It could be very expensive to furnish," she warned.

"Since I plan to be doing a great deal of business entertaining, I view it as an investment. One that's a lot more appealing than some of the blue-chip Fortune Five Hundred stocks my broker keeps selling me."

"There's something to be said for blue-chip stocks," Bliss murmured, thinking of Zelda's nest egg. The one Alan had stolen and Michael, bless him, had recovered.

"They're boring."

"And you're not a man who likes being bored," she suggested.

"You called that one right."

Unlike the French-style houses in the Quarter, set flush to the sidewalk, but boasting hidden courtyards in back, the magnificent mansions in the Garden District had been built back from the street in true American style, their lush green and flower-bedded front yards bordered by hedges, walls and fences.

Shayne stopped in front of a lacy cast-iron gate on tree-lined Prytania Street.

"We're home," he announced as he lowered his window, leaned out and punched a series of numbers into the box embedded in a brick pillar. A moment later the gate opened.

"This is this your house?" She stared in awe at the palatial mansion built in the eclectic blend of Greek Revival and Italianate styles that had been so popular in the booming South before the Civil War.

"Something wrong with it?"

He paused again between another set of pillars set on either side of the cobblestone driveway a long distance from the street. The electric eyes scanned the car, then opened the door to an oversize garage that could easily hold three cars with room to spare.

"It's so—" her mind was whirling "—huge."

"I told you it was." Shayne pulled the Jag into the garage; the door closed behind them. "Are you saying you're not up to the challenge?"

She tilted her chin and stiffened her spine. "Not at all. It's just that I wasn't expecting anything quite so grand." A terrible thought occurred to her. "What's it like inside?"

"You're about to see. But don't worry, it's not a wreck. The previous owners had it restored. All it needs now is someone who knows how to return the interior to its glorious past."

He got out of the car, shut his door and came around to open hers. After she'd climbed out of the front seat, he lifted a wicker basket from the back, then punched another code on the box beside the door leading from the garage into the house.

"You certainly have enough security," she murmured.

"You can't be too careful. No telling when some cat burglar or jewel thief might decide to pay a visit."

He was looking down at her, something unreadable glittering in his crystal blue eyes. If she hadn't known better, she'd have thought Shayne was angry with her.

"That's a frightening idea. It's bad enough worrying about thieves breaking into the shop. I don't think I'd be able to sleep at night worrying about someone breaking into my home."

"It's not exactly a pleasant thought," he agreed dryly, deciding that she was in the wrong business. If she ever decided to give up filching diamonds for a living, she could always turn to acting. She'd be a sure winner for best performance by a sweet-smelling jewel thief.

The door opened on to a wide double parlor, resplendent with soaring ceilings that appeared to be at least fifteen feet high, exquisitely carved moldings, and a mural depicting life in the Antebellum South that ran around the entire length of the room above the chair rail.

"Oh!" Bliss stared around in wonder. "It's magnificent."

"It's also empty." He didn't mention that Cunningham had been less than pleased at the idea of stripping the government safe house of furniture on such short notice. "Which is where you come in. If you decide to accept the assignment."

"I'd be crazy not to."

She walked across the gleaming mahogany floor, through the arched doorway festooned with plaster detailing, to a marble-floored foyer. The focal point of the foyer was a magnificent, curved double stairway.

Furnishing Shayne Broussard's Garden District home could solve all her financial difficulties. On the other hand, she reminded herself, the job would put her in constant contact with a man who already was providing more temptation than was safe.

Deciding to think about all this later, Bliss opted to relax and enjoy the moment. And the company. "Why don't you show me the rest of the house?"

"After lunch. There's gotta be at least thirty stairs to the second floor...I wouldn't want you swooning from hunger, falling down and breaking your lovely neck."

When he brushed a finger over the nape of her neck, Bliss couldn't restrain the slight shiver. He was suddenly too close for comfort.

She stepped back. "I told you, I've never swooned in my life."

"Good for you. Let's try to keep it that way."

He was carrying the basket in his left hand. Linking the fingers of his right with hers, he led her through another arched doorway. "I thought it'd seem more like a picnic if we ate outside."

The walled garden was a riot of bright, colorful blooms—hollyhocks, roses, larkspur, rain lilies and foxglove.

"This truly is lovely," Bliss said as a soft breeze wafted past her, carrying the scent of flowers. Fat bees buzzed around the blooms, butterflies flitted from blossom to blossom. "I'm glad I let you talk me into it."

Bliss, who couldn't help but be enchanted, began thinking of ways to bring the garden look indoors. The house was so large, so formal, floral prints and live plants would make it seem more livable. More of a home.

Shayne paused in the act of unpacking the wicker basket to drink in the sight of her wind-ruffled bright curls, her green, pleasure-filled eyes, wider and softer, more innocent than any thief's eyes had a right to be. Her lips were full and pink, and tilted in a smile as they currently were, made him want to kiss her senseless.

He wanted to touch her—to tangle his fingers in her hair, to run the back of his hand down her cheek, to cup her too strong chin in his fingers and claim her mouth with his own. He wanted to strip that emerald green silk blouse and short pleated skirt from her and drag her down onto the floral printed cushions of that white wrought iron garden bench and...

When he found his fantasies once again getting too X-rated for comfort, when he felt his heated-up body start to overrule the cool logic of his mind, Shayne reminded himself, yet again, that she was not only an assignment, but a suspect.

The chef at the hotel had outdone herself, providing a fresh green salad topped with avocado and artichoke hearts, spicy shrimp packed away in an insulated container, chocolate éclairs, and a bottle of champagne.

Bliss arched a brow as he opened the dark green bottle with an ease that suggested a great deal of practice. "What are we celebrating?"

He poured the champagne into the flutes the chef had packed along with the picnic lunch and handed one to her. "Take your choice. A successful collaboration—"

"I haven't agreed to work with you, yet." But she would, she knew. The temptation of this lovely home, not to mention the money involved, was irresistible.

"Then reunions." He touched the tip of his glass to

hers. "I've thought about you, Bliss Fortune. More than I should. More than I'd expected to."

Her step backward was instinctive. As was the hand that went up to press against his chest. "You don't sound very happy about that."

"I'm not accustomed to women messing up my mind and interfering with my work."

His voice was tinged with the soft vowels of the South, reminding her that she knew nothing about this man. "Where are you from?" she asked suddenly.

A shutter went down over his eyes. "Here and there." She could feel him emotionally distancing himself.

"That's really not much of an answer."

Tough. Because it's all you're going to get, Shayne said silently. "We moved around a lot when I was a kid. I never really felt like any place was home." It was definitely time to change the subject. "If you don't want to drink to collaborations or reunions, how about to us?"

"I told you—"

"I know. There isn't going to be an us. But at least we can agree to be friends. After all, Mike O'Malley did vouch for me."

And Michael was, Bliss reminded herself, more than a mere tenant. He was a true friend. Perhaps the best she'd ever had, which was why it bothered her that he didn't have any woman in his life.

As she thought, not for the first time, that such a warm, kindhearted man as Michael O'Malley should have a loving wife and a houseful of children, Bliss wished that he stirred even the slightest desire in her. Or she, in him. Although she'd sworn off men after her divorce, she couldn't deny that the idea of being loved by such an honest, dependable, sexy man was more than appealing.

And speaking of sexy... As Shayne's gaze settled on her lips, Bliss's breath backed up in her throat and lungs.

He trailed the fingers of his free hand up her arm and decided her skin reminded him of rose petals.

"You realize, of course, that you're driving me crazy."

"Oh?" She wished she sounded strong and sure and not so breathless.

"Here's the deal." His own voice sounded strained and rough as he put his glass slowly, significantly down on the table. "I'm giving you fair warning, Bliss. If you don't tell me to leave you alone right now, I'm going to kiss you." His free arm curved around her waist, drawing her close enough that she could feel the heat from his body seeping into hers.

She should do exactly that. She should put her champagne glass on the table next to his and run away from this man and the dangerous temptation he represented.

That's what she should do, of course. But then again, as Zelda had pointed out on more than one occasion, sometimes it was very difficult to take one's own good advice.

She thought it said something positive about Shayne's innate honesty that he'd given her fair warning, rather than just taking what he wanted without any consideration for her own feelings. Especially since she knew that she wasn't fooling either of them. She didn't accept this luncheon invitation today because she was hungry for spicy shrimp.

"Time's up."

Unlike the first time, when his lips had been cool, the kiss brief, his mouth claimed hers with a hot, hungry passion that created an instantaneous flare of heat.

He didn't coax her into the mists, he dragged her weak-kneed into the flames. His lips didn't tease or tantalize, they plundered, frightening her even as they made her want more.

Her body flamed, her mind emptied. She wrapped her arms around his waist, vaguely aware on some distant level of the sound of crystal shattering on brick as she clung to him, her hands fretting up and down his back, reveling in the feel of taut muscle beneath her fingertips.

She felt so soft. So warm. So willing. Shayne pulled her closer, pressing her slender body against his in a way that set a series of chain reactions rioting through him. Her lips were silk and avid beneath his; she welcomed the invasion of his tongue, answering it with a sensual dance of her own.

His hot mouth ravaged her throat in a blaze of passion, and he was rewarded when she gasped out his name and clung harder, tilting her head back, inviting his possession.

Her arched back lifted her breasts in a way that made him want her. Made him crave her. It took all the self-control he possessed not to rip that emerald silk away, but instead he brushed his palms against the soft yielding flesh, satisfied when he felt her nipples stiffen to a diamond hardness.

"Shayne..."

"It's all right, sugar." He pulled the blouse free of the skirt's waistband. "Don't worry, I won't hurt you."

A dark, dangerous desire unlike anything she'd ever experienced surged through her veins, bringing with it an edge of fear Bliss found both exciting and terrifying. She'd never felt like this in her life; she hadn't known it was even possible for one woman to feel so much. And still need more.

"Shayne..." Her planned words stuck in her throat.

She swallowed painfully and tried again. "Please...I don't think..."

"That's right," he encouraged, his tongue creating wet havoc at an ear she'd never realized possessed a direct link to that hot aching place between her legs. "Don't think, darlin'. Just feel." He dragged her even closer against him, allowing her to experience the full extent of his arousal.

Her mind reeling from the primal demands of her body, Bliss heard a pained, ragged moan and realized it had been ripped from her own throat. She felt her body hum, her knees weaken.

"Shayne," she repeated on a gasp as he caught a nipple between a thumb and forefinger and tugged almost painfully. "Please...don't...I can't."

His blood was pounding in his ears. His body felt on the verge of exploding and what he'd always considered his ironclad control was deserting him, as if it had been melted away by the heated demands of their bodies. But when he heard her soft plea, he managed, just barely, to drag himself back from the brink.

He took in a deep draught of air and looked down into her lovely, larcenous face. "I think you mean that."

"I do." Her cheeks flamed even hotter as she was forced to acknowledge exactly how outrageously she'd behaved. "I never meant for things to get so out of hand so quickly."

"Believe me, darlin', if you give me a chance, I promise to take things real slow from here on in."

There it was again, that slow drawl that reminded her of warmed molasses. It lapped against the flimsy ramparts of her self-control like a rising river threatening the levee.

She combed a hand through her hair. "I can't get in-volved with you," she insisted.

He caught the trembling hand on its second pass and brought it to his lips. "Can't?" He kissed her fingertips, one at a time. "Or won't?"

Feeling herself slipping beneath the warm waters of seduction again, she jerked her hand away. "Can't, won't, it doesn't really matter, does it? Since either way, the answer's no."

He gave her a long deep look. "You're right, of course," he said finally, just when her nerves were about to shatter. "I was brought up to understand that when a lady says no—for whatever reason—a guy backs off."

She was wondering why she was faintly disappointed that he was surrendering his seduction battle so quickly, when she felt his knuckles brush against the bare flesh of her torso, then realized he was just tucking her wrinkled blouse back into her waistband.

"I promised you lunch."

She stared up at him as if he were suddenly speaking another language. "You still want to eat?"

"I'm starving. And, I suspect, after the day you've had, you're hungry, as well."

"Well, yes, but..." Suddenly uncomfortable with this conversation, she turned her gaze toward the fountain, pretending sudden interest in the sun-gilded water.

"If you think I'm going to hold your changing your mind against you, you should know, right off the bat, that sulking isn't my style."

The edgy hunger in his voice had been replaced by that easygoing humor that had so attracted her to him in the first place. Encouraged and confused, she looked up into his pleasant, but frustratingly unreadable face.

"I don't understand you."

"There's not that much to understand. I'm a normal man, Bliss. With normal desires. When I see a lovely woman who turns me on—" he skimmed the back of his hand up her face "—I want her. It's as simple as that. But I'm not into forcing women...lovemaking works best when the lady in question wants me, too."

He sounded so worldly. So experienced. *So like Alan*, that tiny voice of warning in the back of her mind managed to counsel.

"I'll bet a lot of women have wanted you."

He gave her a quick, charming grin, but watching him carefully as she was, Bliss noticed that it didn't quite reach his eyes. "A gentleman never kisses and tells."

Deciding that it was time—past time—to change the subject, she glanced down at the shards of glass at her feet. "I broke the champagne flute."

"You can have mine." He pressed it into her hand. "Drink up. I think you'll like it. It's the same label we shared in Paris."

"I'm surprised you'd remember."

"I remember everything about that night, Bliss. Including the fact that I've never wanted to take a woman to bed more in my life than I did when I kissed you. Until this afternoon, that is."

This time his smile seemed genuine, lightening his eyes to the hue of a cloudless summer sky. Bliss was confused, attracted, and, dammit, still physically needy.

She took a sip of the sparkling wine for courage, then met his friendly gaze with a worried look of her own. "Do you think it's still possible for us to work together?"

"Of course. So long as you want the job."

"I do. But after what happened..."

"The only thing that happened, darlin', is that we

shared a kiss. One that was, admittedly, more world-tilting than most. But it was only a kiss."

Only a kiss. She imagined that entire galaxies had been blown to smithereens with less force and heat. Still, since he seemed able to take what to her had been an earth-shattering experience in stride, and desperately needing this job, Bliss vowed to try to do likewise.

"You're right." Her smile wobbled slightly, revealing her lingering uneasiness. He touched the neck of the champagne bottle to the rim of her glass and as they both drank to a successful collaboration, Bliss hoped that she wasn't making a fatal mistake.

7

WHILE BLISS WAS sharing her picnic lunch with Shayne, Zelda was glaring up at the man who'd rung her doorbell. "You have a helluva lot of nerve, showing your face around here. If you're looking for Bliss—"

"Actually, it was you I wanted to speak with." With the deft tenacity of an aluminum siding salesman, Alan stuck his buttery-soft Italian loafer in the door, forestalling her from slamming it in his face.

The elderly woman folded her arms across her breasts. "I can't see that we have anything to say to one another. My Southern upbringing doesn't allow me to say what I'd like to to you. And believe me, boy, there's nothing you could possibly say that would interest me."

"How about the little fact that Bliss is in danger?"

"If you're talking about that fellow she met in Paris—"

"She met someone in Paris? Who?"

"I don't know his name. It's just some rich man who took a fancy to her. Which isn't surprising, since she's one helluva catch. Unfortunately, thanks to your shenanigans, she's gun-shy when it comes to getting involved again."

"I didn't mean to hurt her."

"Well, for someone who wasn't meaning to, you did a bang-up job of it. Not to mention stealing my nest egg."

"That wasn't personal."

"No, it's just the way creeps like you make your living."

"Actually, it is," he agreed mildly, appearing unfazed by her unflattering description. "As for Bliss, I'll admit that marrying her was a mistake. I never meant to get in that deep."

"You just meant to seduce her, steal whatever you could get your grubby hands on, and move on."

"That was the plan." Again, he seemed to take her accusation in stride. "Actually, she wasn't really a target, since it was more than a little obvious that she didn't have anything worth stealing.

"But there was something about Bliss. Something so fresh and innocent, that I found myself believing I might be able to change. To become the man she thought I was. The man she deserved me to be."

Zelda looked unimpressed. "That's a right pretty speech, Alan. And I'm sure it works wonders with softhearted females. But my heart is a lot tougher than Bliss's. And I'm not buying what you're selling."

He cursed, took off his sunglasses, and dragged a hand down his face. When he took it away, his features looked uncharacteristically haggard. Closer examination revealed a black eye, a bruised jaw that was turning a sickly yellowish green and a white line around his grimly set lips.

"We need to talk, Zelda."

"I've nothing to say to you."

"I never realized you were such a liar. You undoubtedly have a great deal to say to me. However, recriminations will have to wait. Because this is a matter of life or death."

Zelda snorted. "As if I'd care whether you lived or died."

"It's not my possible death you should be concerned about. But Bliss's."

"What?" Zelda's bright eyes narrowed suspiciously. "So help me God, Alan, if this is another con—"

"I swear, it's not." He glanced around, as if looking for spies. Or potential assassins. "If you'll only trust me..."

"Now there's a concept," Zelda muttered.

"It's not a con," Alan repeated doggedly. "If Bliss is mixed up in what I think she is, her life's in danger. I need you to warn her."

"Why don't you?"

"She won't talk to me."

"And you think I will?"

"Yes." His expression was grim. "Because the one thing we both have in common, Zelda, old girl, whether you want to accept the idea or not, is that we both, in our own way, care about your granddaughter."

She gave him a long, thoughtful look. Then sighed and opened the door wider, inviting him into the cozy little cottage.

"THIS IS TRULY AMAZING!" Bliss wandered from room to room, staring in wonder at this house Shayne Broussard wanted her to furnish. No, she corrected, no one could possibly consider this a mere house. It was a mansion. A dream. And, the answer to all her prayers.

The interior possessed a scale and architectural adornment unimaginable today. Bliss doubted that even Donald Trump or any of the Rockefellers could have afforded such grand attention to detail.

"Is that original?" she asked, staring up at the fresco adorning the arched dining-room ceiling.

"Supposedly. The house was originally built by a tobacco planter who'd moved from Virginia right before the war."

He did not have to mention which war. Having grown up in the South, Bliss knew there was only one conflict of any note or interest—the War Between the States. Or, as Zelda had muttered on one occasion, the war those damn Yankees insisted on calling the Civil War.

"As if there was anything civil about it," Bliss's grandmother had huffed at the time.

"Then it was built after the war?" She ran her fingers over the ornate gold-leaf frame of a mirror that had to be at least ten feet tall.

"During."

"You're kidding." Surprised, she looked over at him, leaning against the molded mantel of the two-way fireplace, arms crossed over his chest.

"He began construction in 1861. Finished it in 1866."

"That's an amazing accomplishment, considering the privations people were suffering in the city at the time."

"I suppose this house is proof of the fact that if you want something badly enough, you can accomplish anything."

"I suppose so."

Her heels tapped on the wood floor that had been polished to a glossy, mirrorlike sheen as she went through an ornately decorated plaster archway into a back parlor where French doors opened to yet another dazzling garden. This one, however, was far more formal, designed in the style of a nineteenth-century French garden, with diamond, circle and star-shaped flower beds bordered by leafy green privet hedges and pea-size stones.

A skirted table would be nice in front of the bay window, Bliss decided. Along with a Victorian gentleman's open armchair and a lady's matching settee. But not the usual velvet, which would be too heavy. Perhaps a nice green damask that would bring in the outdoors. Or better yet, needlework cushions. That idea conjured up a mental picture of a woman of the era dressed in a hoopskirt, sitting in the slanting afternoon sunshine, working on a floral canvas.

"Fascinating," Shayne murmured.

Bliss dragged herself away from her mental picture of a floral Kashmir rug in the center of the room and looked up at him. "What?"

"Watching your mind work. You looked a million miles away."

"More like several decades. I was picturing this house as it might have been."

"And can be again." Having watched her roam the empty rooms, Shayne had felt almost guilty for deceiving her. Jewel thief or not, she definitely loved antiques. "If you take the job."

"I'd love it." A smile bloomed. Anticipation sparkled in her eyes like sunshine on a tropical lagoon, making him want to kiss her senseless.

"I suppose it's only fair to warn you that I believe in a hands-on management style." He slipped those hands in question deep into his pockets to keep them out of trouble.

"What does that mean?"

"It means I'll want to work closely with you. Discuss your plans for each room. Go to auctions or wherever it is you find the furniture and knickknacks that will turn this place from an empty mausoleum into a home."

"We'll need to discuss a budget."

"What if I said whatever it takes?"

She laughed at that. "You've obviously no idea what

you're getting into. With an attitude like that, if I were a dishonest person, I could end up bankrupting you."

He reached out to tuck a stray curl behind her ear. "Lucky for me you're an honest lady."

He was suddenly standing too close. Something Bliss reluctantly recognized as desire skimmed down her spine. She edged away to study a mural of a chateau perched on a hillside somewhere in the French countryside.

"Lucky," she murmured.

Heaven help her, she could still feel the touch of his fingers in that spot behind her ear that she'd never imagined could be so sensitive. Dual feelings of anticipation and apprehension fluttered inside her.

As badly as she admittedly needed this commission, as much as she'd truly love bringing this glorious old house to life, a very strong part of her feared she wouldn't have the strength to avoid falling in love with this man.

She turned, her expression worried. And resolved. "I want the job, Shayne. But that's all I want."

Liar. He wondered if she honestly thought he hadn't picked up on the vibrations that had hummed through her when he'd touched her. Wondered if she believed that it was possible for either one of them to work closely with the other and not keep thinking of that shared kiss. And wanting to repeat it. Again and again.

"I'm disappointed, Bliss."

"Because I'm stating up front that I won't have sex with you to get the job?"

"No. Because you aren't willing to give me the benefit of the doubt. Believe it or not, I'm not in the habit of dragging every woman I do business with off to bed."

She blushed at that. Another soft wash of color that

Shayne found both appealing and disconcerting. It was difficult to keep his objective in mind when that damn innocence he was beginning to suspect was not an act kept popping up.

Feeling like a man walking a tightrope, he crossed the room, stood toe-to-toe with her, and framed her face between his palms. "I'll admit to wanting to go to bed with you, Bliss. But I'm also willing to wait until you want it, too."

That was exactly the problem, she thought miserably. That's precisely what she'd been wanting—been fantasizing about—since that magical, reckless night in Paris.

"It's not that simple."

"No." Truer words had never been spoken. "But I've never trusted simple. Or easy." He traced her top lip with the pad of his thumb. "We'll keep our relationship on a professional level for as long as you want."

She looked up at him, searched his disconcertingly blue eyes for answers and decided that about this, at least, he was telling the truth. "Thank you."

She would be strong, Bliss vowed. Whenever she felt herself slipping under Shayne Broussard's spell, she'd just remember Alan.

As they began walking back through the empty house, their footsteps echoing around them, Shayne linked their fingers together in a casual nonthreatening way.

Just when she began to relax, he revealed an uncanny ability yet again to read her mind.

"When we finally do make love, believe me, sweetheart, you'll forget that rich playboy ex-husband that's got you so spooked ever existed."

It was not, Bliss feared, an idle boast.

SEVEN DAYS AFTER first taking Bliss to the safe house,
Shayne opened the door to his hotel suite to find his
older brother, who, without waiting for an invitation,
walked into the room.

"You realize, of course, that I ought to punch your
lights out."

Shayne paused in the act of taking two imported beers
from the hotel minibar and glanced up. "What did I do
now?"

"Bliss has been walking on air for the past week, planning design boards for all the rooms, going through cat-
alogues, making phone calls to dealers all through the
South, even as far away as Baltimore and New York,
thinking that she's going to be decorating that damn
house of yours."

"Is that all?" Shayne closed his mind to the twinge of
guilt caused by his brother's words, shrugged and
handed Michael one of the bottles. "Hell, I'm not hurting anyone. It's not as if she's had to put out any of her
own money. And I'm reimbursing her for the long-
distance calls."

"She might not be out any money yet. But what about
the auction in New Iberia?"

"I have a generous expense account on this case. I can
afford to buy enough stuff to keep her happy."

"Happy?" Michael unscrewed the cap and took a long
swallow. "That's not exactly the word I'd use. How the
hell do you think she's going to feel when the truth
comes out? That you were using her? And that I was
helping you, dammit."

Observing his brother's obvious frustration, Shayne
felt a stir of something alien deep in his gut. "That's
what's bothering you, isn't it? That I accidentally got
you involved."

"I told you," Michael said grimly, "Bliss is a special woman. I don't want her hurt. The idea that I might have any part in that—no matter how peripheral—is tearing up my insides."

Hell, Shayne realized with unwelcome surprise, that strange feeling was jealousy. He was actually jealous of Mike's close relationship with Bliss.

"Exactly how involved with her are you?"

"We're just friends," he said, echoing Bliss's earlier claim. "But in case it's escaped your attention, some people value friendship as much as they do sex."

"Some people need to get out more."

"Dammit, Shayne!" It was a roar. One Shayne recalled all too well from his youth.

"Last time you yelled at me like that, you proceeded to knock my block off."

"You deserved it. LueAnne Comeaux was only seventeen years old. Even if you overlook the fact that she deserved better than a tumble in the back of your Trans Am, she was jailbait."

"I was only just eighteen myself," Shayne reminded his older brother. "And for the record, she'd been throwing herself at me for six straight weeks. Hell, she even showed up for our date with a condom in her purse."

"You were the guy. It was your responsibility to let her down gently."

"In the first place, no eighteen-year-old hormone-driven kid in his right mind would have turned LueAnne down." And very few had, Shayne remembered as he took a pull on his own beer bottle.

"If she was anything like her sister, LueAnne might have been a little fast," Michael conceded. "Lord knows Roarke got beat up trying to defend the older Comeaux girl's less than pristine honor. But that still didn't make what you did right."

Shayne sighed. "Some things never change. You're as rigid and chauvinistic as ever."

"So I've been told."

"Has anyone told you that women have the vote? And the pill? Not to mention the right to initiate sex these days?"

Michael did not appear at all disturbed by the unflattering suggestion that he was behind the times. Instead, his eyes immediately narrowed, his gaze like a laser as it drilled into his brother's face.

"Are you saying Bliss came on to you?"

"No. That's not what I'm saying. But if she does—hell, if we decide to swing from the Victorian brass chandelier in her precious Treasure Trove, or make mad, passionate love in an antique bathtub in the safe house, it's no one's business but our own."

"I don't want her hurt."

"She's a jewel thief—"

"The hell she is!" Michael slammed the beer bottle down onto the table, causing an explosion of white foam to bubble over the rim. "You've been hanging around The Treasure Trove since you got into town. And you've broken into it every night—yeah, I've watched—" he said in answer to Shayne's surprised look. "So tell me, hotshot, have you found one single shred of evidence that she's what you say she is?"

"No, but—"

"There aren't any buts about it. You haven't found any evidence because none exists. I'm a detective. Don't you think I'd notice if my landlady was involved in something as nefarious as jewel smuggling?"

"You might, if you weren't so prejudiced in her favor.

I've decided she wouldn't be stupid enough to keep the jewels in the shop, and since there's no record of any safe-deposit box, she's obviously got them stashed in her house somewhere. Which is where you come in. She mentioned you were friends with the grandmother—"

"No way." Michael set his jaw in a stubborn line Shayne remembered all too well. "I am not going to help you invade Bliss's privacy. It's bad enough that I haven't told her who—and what—you are."

"If you truly believe she's innocent, you'd think you'd want to help me prove it."

Michael's answering curse was ripe. "I can't believe I'm letting you get me involved in one of your damn scams."

"I'm not asking for a favor. The government's prepared to hire you as a consultant. And believe me, Mike, they're willing to pay well to shut down this ring."

"Bliss Fortune doesn't belong to any damn international jewel theft ring."

Although Shayne was not yet prepared to admit his misgivings, he was admittedly beginning to have his own doubts. During his years working for the Company, he'd learned to recognize all the signs of a person who was not what he or she appeared to be. And try as he might, he couldn't make Bliss fit the profile.

He took another drink of beer, meeting his brother's challenging look. "Then help me prove it."

"Hell." Michael shook his head with self-disgust. "Did you ever think about retiring and settling down in a nice little house with a white picket fence, two-point-five kids and a dog?"

"I've thought about it."

"And?"

"And I decided I'd rather spend the rest of my life in a Turkish prison."

"I seem to remember Roarke saying something along those same lines. And he's real happy living with Daria."

"Good for him. Maybe, when all this is over and I can come out in the open, the four of us can get together and toast his newfound domesticity. Meanwhile, I have a jewel thief to capture. And I could really use your help."

Michael's granite expression could have been carved on the side of Mount Rushmore, but Shayne felt the unwavering fraternal support and knew that however much it cost Mike personally, his brother would come through for him.

"Hell." His tone was flat and held not an iota of enthusiasm. "What kind of cockamamy plan have you come up with this time?"

CAUGHT UP IN her enthusiasm for the largest and most artistically challenging project she'd ever tackled, Bliss was working nearly around the clock. Zelda, unsurprisingly, had been hovering over her like a mother hen, worrying that she wasn't eating properly, or sleeping enough. And then there'd been that strange convoluted story about Alan and jewel thieves and a paste necklace disappearing during the party in Paris.

"It's just another scam," she assured Zelda.

"You didn't see his face, honeybunch." The older woman twisted her hands together. The purple shadows beneath her eyes revealed her own lack of sleep ever since her former grandson-in-law had told her the incredible story. "Somebody beat him up real badly."

"Good." Bliss took a gulp of coffee and peeled a banana, knowing from experience that it was probably the only thing she'd be eating until much later today. She had to drop by the store, then she was going to a plantation house auction in New Iberia with Shayne. "Probably some irate husband whose wife he was fooling around with."

"He says he's worried about you."

"That'll be the day."

Bliss didn't want to talk about her cheating, lying former husband. She didn't want to think about him. Even if it did help her keep her distance from Shayne. Not that she needed any help. Ever since that day at his marvelous house, he'd been an absolute gentleman, not revealing in any way—with looks, words, or touches—that he wanted her.

Perhaps he'd changed his mind, she thought as she put the cup in the dishwasher. That would certainly be conforming to the type of person he was—the rich man who, when he didn't get what he wanted immediately, moved on to the next target.

"I've got to run." She kissed her grandmother's powdered cheek. "Don't wait up for me. I could be late."

"Perhaps you could bring your beau back with you this time," Zelda suggested. "So I could meet him."

"He's not my beau. He's a client."

"So you say." Bliss's grandmother's knowing gaze swept over her. "Carting home antiques can be dirty work. I'm surprised you chose that dress."

Bliss ran her hands down the front of the short skirt. A watercolor garden that could have washed off an impressionist painting bloomed on the silk and was echoed in the boat-necked sleeveless blouse.

"It's cool."

"It's silk."

"That's the point. Silk breathes. Besides," Bliss insisted, "it's washable silk."

"Well, then." Zelda's lips quirked in a smile. "That makes all the difference."

Although she'd felt pretty and confident when she'd chosen her skirt and blouse, by the time Bliss got to The Treasure Trove, she was second-guessing her decision. If Zelda saw through her motives so quickly, what was to stop Shayne from realizing that she'd dressed for him?

"Why don't you make up your damn mind," she muttered, frustrated by her unwanted feelings for the man.

Feelings that were in danger of becoming an obsession. Bliss thought about Shayne Broussard first thing in the morning, when she woke up. She thought about him all during the days, which were growing increasingly steamy as summer approached, and his handsome face and devilish eyes were the last thing she'd see before drifting off into a restless sleep, a sleep tortured with hot, erotic dreams in which Shayne played a starring role.

"It's only natural," she insisted as she put aside a brass kaleidoscope she thought would look nice on the mahogany tripod table she'd found for his library. "He represents the biggest commission you've ever had. This job could catapult you into the big leagues. It's only normal that you'd think about him all the time."

Bliss was so caught up in her emotional and mental turmoil, she didn't hear the silvery tinkle of the bell as the door to the store opened.

"Still talking to yourself, I see," a deep, dreadfully familiar voice said.

She spun around and was surprised when her usual knee-jerk reaction of anger didn't rock through her. Hercules was apparently not as forgiving. He uncurled himself from the wicker basket he'd been dozing in, jumped down onto the floor in front of Alan Fortune, arched his back and hissed.

"Hello, Alan." Another surprise. She could say his name without any danger of choking.

"Hello, Bliss." After scowling back at the cat, which he'd always hated, he glanced around the shop. "This is such a quaint place. It always reminds me of the inside of a Fabergé egg."

"You should know. Since you've undoubtedly stolen one."

"Never had the privilege." He picked up the kaleidoscope and held it up to the front window. "Ever wonder about the appeal of these things?"

"They're fun. And pretty."

"True." He turned the tube, causing the pieces of colored glass to change position. "But I think people like them because they remind them of their own lives. Constantly shifting and changing."

"Is there a point to this, Alan?"

"Actually, there is." He put the kaleidoscope back on the counter. "I came for the jewels, Bliss."

"The jewels?"

"It was a cute practical joke and I've no idea how you pulled it off, especially since I wouldn't have guessed you had a larcenous bone in your lovely little body. But you've made your point. So now it's time to come clean. Before you find yourself landing in prison. Or worse."

"Excuse me?" She lifted a copper brow. "I'm afraid, except for the part about my not being larcenous, the meaning of that statement eludes me."

"Dammit, Bliss." Frustration was etched into every line of his tanned face. A face she'd once thought was handsome. But now, comparing it with Shayne's, she realized it was soft and lacked character. "I realize that I didn't exactly treat you fairly—"

"That's putting it mildly, Alan."

Once again Bliss was surprised when she could discuss his treachery with such inner calm. In the past, just the thought of her former spouse could cause fury to simmer inside her.

"You seduced me, married me before I knew what was happening, was unfaithful the entire time—making a fool of me in front of all your jet-set friends—then you had the unmitigated gall to steal my grandmother's nest egg."

"No one's perfect," he muttered. "What do you want me to do? Admit that I behaved abominably, then get down on my knees and beg your forgiveness?"

"That would be a start." She couldn't help smiling at the image of this suave man on his knees. She also knew it would be as phony as everything else about her former husband. "But it's not necessary. It's over, Alan. Truly over."

She shook her head, surprising herself as much as him. "I used to think about you all the time. I envisioned your flaming car plunging from the Huey P. Long Bridge. I imagined you getting eaten by alligators after your speedboat turned over in the bayou.

"I even once contemplated putting some money on Marie Laveau's tomb and asking her to put a voodoo curse on you. But that's all in the past. I don't think about you, Alan. In fact, it's as if you never existed."

"Dammit, would you quit being so stubborn?" His eyes hardened, but observing him closely, Bliss could detect fear in them. "Didn't Zelda explain the danger?"

"She mentioned something about a necklace and

paste. But to tell you the truth, since I wasn't interested, my mind drifted and I didn't quite get the gist of this latest story."

"It's not a story! Don't you get it? You've been set up."

"By whom?"

"I don't know. I wouldn't have known *that* if Angela didn't talk in her sleep."

"Angela?"

"It's not important." He waved the identity of his latest bedmate away with an impatient hand. "You may be right that I owe you for whatever pain I caused. Which is why I'm risking my own life to warn you that those jewels aren't real. They're part of a trap, dammit." He curved his hands around her shoulders, his fingers digging tightly into the silk-covered skin.

The pain was surprising. Although he'd savagely wounded her heart, and her pride, Alan had never lifted a hand to her.

"You've signed my death warrant, Bliss." Seeming both frustrated and horribly frightened, he shook her. "And you could be next." Another shake, hard enough to make her teeth rattle.

Before she could answer, the door to The Treasure Trove burst open and Alan was literally jerked off his feet and thrown across the room, where he hit the composite cuirassier's suit of armor consisting of seventeenth-century and Victorian pieces she'd bought at a savings and loan bankruptcy auction in Baton Rouge.

"If you even try to get up, I'll break every bone in your body," Shayne said in a voice that reminded Bliss of the low, threatening growl of a wolf. "And if you ever touch this woman again, believe me, I'll kill you. Then cut you into little pieces and feed you to the gators."

He was standing over her former husband, hands

curled into tight fists, menace radiating from every male pore. Bliss didn't know whether to be thrilled or terrified.

"Shayne..." She reached out and put her hand on his arm where muscles had tensed to the hardness of boulders.

"Stay out of this, Bliss."

Without shifting his gaze from Alan, who was lying dazed amidst the scattered pieces of metal, he reached over to the wall, took down a Confederate officer's sword, pulled it from its leather scabbard and pressed the gleaming point against the cowering man's throat.

"Now," he said with a cold smile and a deadly resolve that frightened Bliss, "where were we?"

8

"WHO THE HELL are you?" Alan tried for bluster and failed. His Adam's apple bobbed violently as he swallowed. Hard.

Shayne's eyes were as smooth and cold as an Arctic ice field. "I'm Shayne Broussard, the man who's about to send you to your Maker."

"I've heard of you." A bit of fear faded from wide, terrified eyes. "You're some sort of wheeler-dealer in Europe." As Bliss watched, her former husband began to relax by inches. "You'd never risk prison by committing murder."

"Want to bet?" Shayne's smile belied the picture he made with the gleaming steel point of his sword still pressed against Alan Fortune's throat. "Besides, if you know my reputation, you'll also know that I have powerful friends. Friends who'll ensure that I'd never serve a day in prison for justifiable homicide."

"Justifiable? I was merely having a discussion with my ex-wife when you came bursting into the shop like a madman, threw me against the wall and threatened to kill me. What the hell is justifiable about that?"

"You had your hands on Bliss."

"So?"

"No one touches her but me."

"Ah, hell, is that all this is about? Jealousy? Believe

me, I'm not interested in having sex with her. She's all yours."

Although Bliss was still frightened by Shayne's surprisingly violent behavior, Alan's statement stung. The nerve of the man, to think he possessed the right to so blithely hand her over to another man for sex.

"For your information, Alan Fortune—"

"Stay out of this, Bliss," Shayne interrupted in a quiet voice. "This is between Fortune and myself."

"You're just as bad as he is." Her frustrated breath ruffled her bright bangs. "In case you haven't noticed, Shayne, this just happens to be between me and my former cheating, lying, stealing, rat of a spouse."

"Why don't you tell me how you really feel about me?" Alan asked dryly.

"She's right. So shut up." Shayne pressed the sword a little deeper, drawing a scarlet bead of blood.

All assurance Alan had managed to recapture instantly fled. "Dammit, let me go. You're a crazy man, Broussard."

A deep voice entered the conversation. "I'll second that." Three pairs of eyes immediately cut to where Michael was filling the doorway of The Treasure Trove. "Since I assume you all aren't staging a reenactment of the battle scenes from *Gone with the Wind* or *Captain Blood*, does someone want to tell me what's going on?"

"This weasel was threatening Bliss," Shayne said.

"What is he, suicidal? Or just stupid?"

"My guess would be both."

"It really wasn't anything," Bliss began earnestly, worried at the way her tenant's eyes had turned as dark and dangerous as Shayne's. Once again she was struck by the resemblance between the two men, although this time she noticed that Michael, who'd always seemed so nice and easygoing, appeared even more dangerous than Shayne.

"He also laid hands on her," Shayne continued the explanation, ignoring Bliss's attempt at soothing the waters.

"Well, hell." Michael's hand went to his shoulder holster. "I think we ought to take him out in the bayou and shoot him."

"Good try, fellas," Alan said, attempting the feigned cheer that had always made him such a good con man. "You've scared the hell out of me and taught me a lesson. You've won this round."

Shayne and Michael exchanged a look. Then Michael nodded, as if in silent agreement to some unspoken suggestion.

"I don't think you understand," Shayne explained patiently. "The entire point is to ensure that there aren't any more rounds."

"Which is why we have to kill you," Michael said.

Certain that they didn't really mean it, that she couldn't be such a horrendous judge of character to not only misjudge her own former husband, but her friend and tenant and the man she feared she was falling in love with, Bliss decided to relax and enjoy the show.

"You're kidding, right?" Alan's voice held a tremor as his nervous gaze went back and forth between both men who were towering over him.

"I never kid about killing," Shayne said in that same pleasant voice that suggested they were merely engaging in some polite social conversation. "But I'd hate it to be said that I don't give a man a fair chance."

"But the guy's a weasel," Michael said, reaching again for his pistol.

"I realize that." Shayne sighed. "But I'm afraid, if I

have a flaw, it's that I'm a fair-minded man. Which is why I'm tempted to give him an even chance."

Michael made a sound of pure disgust. "I still think we just ought to take him out and shoot him."

"As attractive a scenario as that is, I believe I have a better idea." Shayne glanced at the wall where more swords were on display, then back down at Alan, whose complexion was beginning to fade again to an unhealthy shade of gray. "Have you ever heard about Dueling Oaks?"

"In the park? Where idiots used to duel to the death over what they considered honor?" Alan's scathing tone suggested what he thought of that outdated concept.

"Exactly." Shayne nodded. "I've always thought it might be amusing to fight a duel."

"Over a woman's honor," Michael agreed, picking up his cue with perfect timing.

Shayne lifted the sword from Alan's neck and swished it through the air a few times. "This has a really nice feel to it. You know, I love watching those old swashbuckler movies on late-night cable." He sighed. "I think I may have been born a century too late."

"Or you could have been a pirate in another life," Michael suggested.

"Now there's a thought." Shayne looked down at Alan again, studying him thoughtfully. "Unfortunately, we don't have a plank for you to walk." He switched the sword from hand to hand as he appeared to be considering his options. "I suppose, times being what they are, I'm going to have to let you go."

Never one to miss an opportunity, Alan scrambled to his feet, scattering pieces of armor. But he also seemed unwilling to leave without a final parting shot.

"I wasn't lying, Bliss," he said over his shoulder. "We're talking life or death, here."

With that he was gone.

Watching him practically run across Magazine Street, Bliss missed the look exchanged by the two brothers.

"What was he talking about?" Michael asked.

"I don't know, really," Bliss hedged.

It was bad enough that Michael already knew she'd gotten involved with a con man. She hated for either of them to know that Alan was somehow trying to link her to the theft of some necklace. Since, from what she'd been able to tell from Zelda's convoluted story, the stones had been paste in the first place, she couldn't see that it was really that big a problem. Obviously, Alan had some scam going and she decided that the best thing to do was just to continue to ignore him.

"He said it was life or death," Shayne persisted as Hercules began weaving between his legs, purring with something that resembled feline bliss. Not trusting the mercurial cat, who seemed to be begging to be petted, Shayne did not risk his hand again.

"That's Alan, always exaggerating." Bliss flashed him a bright false smile. "I still wonder what on earth I ever thought I saw in that man."

Wanting to put the unpleasant matter behind her, she went up on her toes and kissed Michael's cheek. "Although it undoubtedly makes me a terrible person, I have to admit I enjoyed watching his face when you threatened to shoot him. Thank you."

Michael's smile didn't meet his eyes, which remained concerned. "It was my pleasure."

"And you were magnificent." She crossed the room to Shayne. "Even if you did wreck a lovely suit of armor."

She'd aimed the kiss at his cheek, as well, but he

turned his head and captured her mouth. Conquered it. The kiss didn't last long. But it still made her blood burn and her mind blur.

"Put it on my bill," he said when the hot, breath-stealing kiss ended.

"I thought you two had an auction to attend in New Iberia." Lilah had arrived at the shop and was staring at the couple.

"We do." Bliss took a huge gulp of air and damned the fire she could feel burning in her cheeks. "In fact, if we don't get going now, we'll be late." She stepped over the metal helmet and was on her way out of the shop when she realized Shayne wasn't following her. "Are you coming?"

He'd been enjoying watching the sway of her hips in that silk skirt, wondering when he'd become such a masochist. If she'd been any other woman, he would have taken her to bed days ago. Hell, probably that first night in Paris. It wouldn't have been that hard. A few long deep kisses, some lingering caresses, pretty words whispered in her ear.

The part of him that had always been willing to do whatever it took to break a case kept reminding Shayne that it'd be a lot easier to keep an eye on Bliss if they were sleeping together, spending not just their days, but their nights under the same roof.

Another part of him—some strange, unsettled alien part he'd never known was lurking inside him—kept thinking that she was different. She might indeed be a thief—and her former husband's appearance in the shop today was certainly damning evidence against her—but she still affected him like no other woman he'd known.

He wanted her for more than just sex. But unaccustomed to introspection when it came to the women in his life, Shayne couldn't get a handle on what he was feeling.

"I'm right behind you," he said, putting the vexing problem behind him for now.

Michael and Lilah watched them leave the shop together, both noticing the easy, possessive touch of Shayne's hands on her hip as they crossed the street to where he'd parked the Jaguar.

"What was that all about?" Lilah asked.

Michael shrugged. "Beats me." But the concern in his eyes deepened as he watched two of the people he cared most about in the world drive away.

AS THEY DROVE away from the city, deep into the bayou, Shayne observed the garish strip centers occupied by the ubiquitous fast-food restaurants that had even cloned themselves all over Europe and thought about how much had changed since he'd left home.

So much around him had changed. But what was deep inside him had changed, as well, he realized. He was not the same young man who'd left Louisiana in search of action, adventure and intrigue. In those days, everything in the world had seemed new and exciting, as glittering and foreign as the Emerald City of Oz.

Over the past decade, he'd drunk coffee and nearly had his neck slit in Ankara, evaded Serb blockades in Bosnia, gotten drunk on ouzo with a sexy blond AP reporter on the Greek isle of Seriphos, watched the sun come up behind the magnificent snow-covered Mount Kilimanjaro that hovered over Tanzania, and made mad, passionate love to a dark-eyed beauty in a Bedouin tent beneath a dazzling white moon in the desert of Abu Dhabi.

He had, Shayne realized now, become jaded, a dispassionate collector of adventures, cities, and, yes, even women, the way tourists collect tacky T-shirts and local crafts as souvenirs of their summer vacations.

And then he'd made the mistake of walking along the Left Bank with a woman who was forcing him to take a long hard look at his life; not only where he'd come from, but who he'd become. And, where he was going.

"This is such amazing country," Bliss murmured as they drove deeper and deeper into the mysterious wetlands, leaving civilization behind them.

He'd left the top down on the Jag; the air rushing by them carried the scent of sugarcane, moss-draped cypress trees and wet green lichen along with the fragrance of the bright yellow four-o'clocks that were still open in lingering puddles of shade.

"It's another world, all right," he agreed as they passed two adolescent boys in a pirogue and experienced a flash of bittersweet memory of youthful crawfish trapping with Roarke and Mike.

"Have you ever been here before?"

"Yes." He didn't—couldn't—elaborate.

"My grandfather was Cajun," she revealed. "He inherited his parents' house on the Bayou Teche. Some of my fondest memories are of the summers I spent there."

There was already too much to like about this woman. To discover they shared an ancestry made her even more dangerous. And appealing.

"But you lived in the city the rest of the time?"

"Yes. Grandpère Dupree was a career navy man. When he retired, he settled down in New Orleans and opened a restaurant. But that didn't last long."

"It's a tough business."

"Especially if you give meals away to every homeless person who shows up at your back door."

"Generosity and good business practices are probably often contradictory."

"I suppose so." Bliss brushed some windblown curls out her eyes. "But I'd much rather be proud of my grandfather Dupree's generous heart than rich. And it's because of him that I got into the antique business. Zelda furnished our house from weekend flea markets. I learned early on how to find treasures in the midst of a lot of trash."

Shayne wanted to believe her. But experience had taught him not to trust. "You might not care about being rich, but those diamonds you were wearing in Paris didn't exactly belong to a pauper."

"They were my mother's."

There was something new in her voice. Something that sounded a lot like pain. And regret.

"So she must have married rich?"

"Actually, she never married." Bliss turned toward him and although he couldn't see her eyes through the tinted lenses of her sunglasses, Shayne could feel the challenge in her gaze. "Which, as the kids in school always loved to point out, technically makes me a bastard."

Shayne shrugged. "I've never been fond of labels."

Yet another lie. In his business everyone got put into neat, tidy pigeonholes. It was the only way a guy stayed alive. And even then he had the scars to prove that sometimes mistakes were made.

"It must have been tough for you, growing up."

"Sometimes." It was Bliss's turn to shrug. "Mama was sick a lot, so I spent most of my time with my grandmother Zelda." She sighed and shook her head. "That's not true. Mama wasn't sick. She was an alcoholic."

"I'm sorry," Shayne said, meaning it.

He wondered if her painful childhood was the reason for her adult criminal behavior, then reminded himself that lots of kids—including his brothers and himself—grew up in untraditional homes and didn't turn out to be international jewel thieves.

"It wasn't as bad as it sounds. She wasn't one of those dramatic, technicolor drunks. She was quiet and wispy, almost like a ghost living in the house."

"You said was."

"She died when I was fourteen."

"I'm sorry," he said again.

"So was I." Again, Bliss thought about how fortunate she'd been to have Zelda. And Dupree, who may have failed at every business he'd attempted, but had ensured that she'd grown up in a home filled with unconditional love.

"I'm surprised you haven't sold the diamonds."

"Why would I do that?"

"Other than the fact that you apparently could use the money, I'd think they'd come with unpleasant memories."

"Oh, no. It's just the opposite. Whenever I wear them, they remind me that there'd been a time before I was born—no matter how brief—when my mother had been in love. When she'd been happy. And that makes me feel close to her."

Once again, Shayne thought that Bliss appeared to be a woman totally without guile. Again, he thought of his brother's assertion that she couldn't possibly be guilty of the crimes she was accused of. Then he glanced down at her smooth tan thighs and thought about how, thief or not, if he didn't make love to her soon, he'd go nuts. Or explode.

"I think I'd like to meet your grandmother," he said.

She laughed at that. "I don't think you're going to have any choice. Zelda told me today that if I didn't invite you for Sunday dinner, she was going to track you down herself."

"That sounds great."

Since Michael had refused to help with that part of the plan, opting instead to do background checks on everyone Alan Fortune had been hanging out with lately, Shayne had been looking for a way to get into Bliss's house.

Since the old lady seemed to spend most of her days puttering around the garden, breaking into it during the day had been out of the question. And since too many things could go wrong in the dark—witness his almost shooting his own brother—he'd never been overly fond of nighttime break-ins.

"I suppose I should warn you that Zelda's an unrelenting matchmaker," Bliss said with forced casualness.

"Terrific." When she glanced over at him in obvious surprise, Shayne shot her a rakish grin. "Just because I promised not to try to seduce you, doesn't mean that I don't still want you, Bliss. I could use someone on my side."

"Wanting is easy," she murmured, watching the tupelo trees flash by. "Too easy, sometimes."

"Agreed. But there's one thing you need to remember, Bliss."

She turned, responding to the steel in his voice. "What?"

"I'm not Alan Fortune."

"I know that." As if needing some physical connection, she placed a hand on his leg.

Shayne, who could feel the imprint of each individual finger burning through the denim of his jeans into the flesh of his thigh, wondered if she knew the impact of such a touch and decided that the gesture, like so much else about Bliss, was impulsive.

"Whatever's happening between us, Shayne, I know that you'd never lie to me the way Alan did."

Shayne reminded himself that he wasn't at all like that slug of an ex-husband. That he was only doing his job. That she'd created the damn situation in the first place by somehow getting herself mixed up with smugglers and thieves.

But as the sun rose higher in the sky, casting a pearly glow over the dark water on either side of the highway, he felt something he had experienced too often lately—a nagging twinge of guilt.

9

THE AUCTION WAS being held in an old plantation house that predated the Civil War and had definitely seen better days. It reminded Shayne of the crumbling, vine-covered ones he'd explored as a kid with Roarke, when each of them had tried to scare the other with tall tales of invisible weeping women and ghosts dressed in Confederate gray and Union blue.

"Isn't this lovely?" Bliss asked as they made their way gingerly up the teetering brick path to the front gallery.

He glanced down at the sawdust running along the crumbling foundation. "It's about to collapse into the bayou."

"It just needs a little care. And someone to love it."

"What it needs is a wrecking ball. The place is a smorgasbord for termites, Bliss."

"I'm certain an exterminator could take care of that little problem." She glanced at the abandoned rice fields behind the house. "I wonder how much land comes with it."

"Surely you're not thinking of buying it?" Since he knew her bank account down to the last dollar, it crossed his mind that she'd have to steal a helluva lot of diamond earrings to even shore up the dangerously unstable foundation.

"Not really." She ran a hand up one of the fluted front columns. "But it's a lovely fantasy."

Watching her stroking touch was all it took to make him hard. *Soon*, Shayne vowed. "So, have you always had this tendency to look at the world through rose-colored glasses?"

"I'm afraid so." The house was shaded by an ancient oak, allowing her to take off her sunglasses. Her eyes, as she looked up at him, were earnest. "You make it sound like a flaw."

"It's just a good way to get into trouble."

"I know." She sighed as she thought about Alan. "But I'd still rather go through life expecting the best from people and sometimes being disappointed, than constantly thinking the worst."

Always expecting the worst was exactly how he'd lived the past ten years, Shayne realized. He'd had the adventures he'd wished for when he'd left Louisiana, but at what price?

"That's not such a bad philosophy, in theory." He hooked his arm around her waist and drew her a little closer. "So, when you think of me—" he ran the back of his free hand down her face, trailing his fingers around her jaw "—do you expect the best?"

Never one to lie—especially to herself—Bliss had long ago accepted that like her grandmother and mother before her, she was destined to go through life leading with her heart. Even her disastrous marriage hadn't changed her romantic nature, which is why, as she watched the warmth deepen Shayne's disconcerting blue eyes, she had no choice but to answer honestly.

"Yes."

A wealth of passion shimmered in that single word, letting Shayne know that the waiting had finally come to an end. "Can I take that to mean that I'm not the only one waking up in a sweat these days?" He toyed with a silky curl.

His touch, casual but intimate, his seductive gaze, the enticing curve of his lips all conspired to make her go weak at the knees. Despite the humidity hanging over the bayou like Spanish moss, her mouth had gone horribly dry.

"No. You're not."

As she looked up at him, her open, honest heart in her eyes, Shayne knew that Michael had been right all along. This woman was no more a jewel thief than he was. Which meant, he realized, that Alan Fortune may have actually been trying to tell the truth about Bliss's life being in danger.

He was going to have to tell her the truth, he decided. It was the best way to debrief her, to discover what the hell was going on. And, possibly, to save her life.

"We need to talk."

She smiled at that. "Funny, I didn't get the impression that talking was at the top of the list of things you wanted to do with me."

"Bliss." Talk about bad timing. She'd finally succumbed, was willing to let him take her off to the nearest bed, and suddenly he was the one changing gears. "Nothing's changed about that. In fact, I want you more than ever. But there are things—"

Shayne broke off his planned explanation as he felt someone coming up behind him.

"Well, well," a smoothly modulated voice said, "imagine seeing you here, Bliss, dear. I would have thought our little contest in Lafayette would have put you off auctions altogether."

Shayne felt Bliss stiffen. "I've no idea what you mean, Nigel," she said, her smooth tone edged with an acid he'd never heard in her voice before. Not even when talking about her ex-husband.

"We've had this discussion before, dear. There's no way you're going to be able to compete in an increasingly competitive marketplace. You're too underfinanced."

"Sorry, pal," Shayne said, breaking into the conversation, "but you've got it backward."

The rival antique dealer arched an aristocratic brow. "I don't believe we've met. I'm Nigel Churchill. And you are...?"

"Shayne Broussard."

"Ah." He nodded thoughtfully. "The mystery man everyone's buzzing about. I'd heard that Bliss had landed you as a client, but since rumors run rampant in this business, I'd dismissed them."

"In this case, they happen to be true. Bliss is furnishing my new home."

"Well, when you're finished playing with amateurs, you may want to give me a call." He reached into a leather case and took out a gray pasteboard card. "I'm sure a man in your position is accustomed to dealing with the best."

"You called that one right. Which is why I came to Bliss. Who is, by the way, far from an amateur. And you may as well head on back to whatever slimy rock you crawled out from under, Churchill old man. Because you're looking at the man who's going to outbid you for every damn piece you came here to buy today."

Having watched Shayne threaten Alan with that sword, Bliss came to the conclusion that he was the type who felt the need to rescue damsels in distress. And, as much as she appreciated having a champion, she couldn't allow him to bankrupt himself just to defend her honor.

"Shayne..."

"Don't worry, darling," he said. "I know what I'm doing."

Although she found the idea of treating her nemesis to some of his own medicine appealing, Bliss couldn't forget the seemingly unlimited funds Nigel had displayed the last time they'd bid against each other.

"I sure hope so," she murmured as she allowed Shayne to lead her into the house where the auction was being held.

A HOT, STEAMY four hours later, Bliss was staring at Shayne in disbelief. "I don't believe it! We got everything we wanted!"

"I told you I knew what I was doing."

Shayne didn't know which he'd enjoyed more—imagining Cunningham's expression when he got the bill for today, or watching the excitement blaze in Bliss's remarkable eyes as the bidding war between he and Nigel Churchill had escalated to a take-no-prisoners intensity.

"But it cost you a fortune." She'd known he was rich; she'd just never guessed how rich.

"I needed furniture. And that jerk needed to be taught a lesson about ethical business practices."

He glanced over at the no longer so smug antique dealer who'd left the plantation house and was standing beside his Rolls-Royce Corniche, engaged in what appeared to be an intense conversation with a thirty-something brunette who looked vaguely familiar.

Shayne decided the government had spent a great deal more money on a lot less admirable pursuits. Besides, he'd enjoyed frustrating the antique dealer who'd obviously given Bliss such grief. By the time he'd paid triple the asking price for that silly-looking piece of furniture Bliss had told him was a fainting couch, the smoke had practically been coming from the top of the other man's head.

Bliss thought about all they'd managed to buy today—the hand-carved mantel, the French doré clock, the Napoleon III black-lacquered chair, the Regency bench, not to mention that darling ivory satin-covered fainting couch that would look so wonderful in the upstairs dressing room, and felt a surge of satisfaction.

She'd even managed to pick up a few things for her own shop when Nigel, who'd finally realized that Shayne intended to live up to his threat, had begun to back off.

"I feel like celebrating," she said.

"You read my mind." He looped his arms around her waist. "How about going somewhere fancy for dinner?"

Looking up at him, Bliss decided that the time for pretending had passed. It was time to admit that she was hungry. But not for food.

"Actually, I think I'd rather share a private celebration." Her voice was soft, her meaning crystal clear.

"I want you to be very certain about this, Bliss."

"I am."

Hell. What was wrong with him? A stunningly gorgeous woman had just offered herself to him and what happened? He was struck with an attack of ethics he hadn't even known he possessed until now.

"You know I've wanted to make love with you from that first night."

She nodded, trying to read his inscrutable face for some clue of what he was about to say. It had taken all her nerve to make the offer in the first place. If he turned it down...

"And I've wanted you to make love to me."

Once again it crossed his mind that his initial impression was right. She truly was the most open, guileless individual he'd ever met. No wonder Fortune had been able to do such a number on her.

"With." At her questioning look, he said, "There is a difference."

Her answering smile lit up her eyes and made her face appear almost translucent. "Yes."

Once again Shayne was sorely tempted to drag her off to the nearest motel. Once again he felt an uncharacteristic need to be honest. Or, at least as truthful as he could under the circumstances.

"The thing is, I have the feeling that you're a forever kind of woman. And I can't offer you that, Bliss."

Even as she felt her open heart plummet, Bliss thought how different this man was from her former husband. Alan had lied from the moment they'd met. Shayne, on the other hand, had proven unflinchingly honest. She thought yet again how much this man reminded her of Michael O'Malley. In more than just looks.

"I understand." Her smile only wobbled slightly. "I'm not asking for forever, Shayne." But, oh, how she wanted that! "We'll just take things one day—and night—at a time."

Torn between conflicting emotions—Lord, where the hell had this damned conscience come from?—Shayne weighed his options. Although he knew he was being self-serving, he told himself that he'd risk hurting her feelings and embarrassing her if he turned her down.

"Let me go pay for the things we bought and arrange to have them delivered," he said. "Then we'll leave."

Bliss let out a deep breath. "I'll wait in the car." Then, mindless of the fact that they were in a public place, she went up on her toes and brushed her lips against his in a light kiss that promised so much more.

After giving her the keys, Shayne watched her walk back to the Jag, his mind concentrating for once, not on that nice rounded bottom, but on her heart. He knew that if he ended up hurting her—which he now seemed destined to do whether he took her to bed or not—Michael would kill him. Which wouldn't be nearly as painful as the disgust he'd feel for himself.

Cursing under his breath at this box he seemed to have nailed himself into, Shayne pulled out the platinum Amex card and went off to spend more of Uncle Sam's money.

BLISS WAS LITERALLY shimmering with anticipation. She felt it humming through her veins, like electricity. As they drove away from the plantation house, she realized that it was indeed possible to feel furnace-hot and ice-cold both at the same time.

"I'd take you to my place," Shayne said, "but there's no furniture, and although I'm willing to take you any way I can get you, I think a bed might be a nice touch."

Bliss was definitely unaccustomed to discussing sex so casually. "My place is out," she murmured, wondering what Zelda would do if she showed up with this man in tow, then disappeared into her bedroom. Probably sing hosannas, and bake the pineapple-pecan upside-down cake she always served for special occasions.

"I could take you to my hotel, but that's so impersonal."

Bliss was relieved at his reluctance to go back to his room. Having gone to school with Thelma London, who was the night manager at the Whitfield Palace Hotel and a horrendous gossip, she knew that by morning the entire town would know that Bliss Fortune was sleeping with her client.

She forced a light laugh that didn't sound nearly as carefree as she'd hoped. "Why do I feel like a teenager, trying to find someplace to park to make out?"

He laughed as well as memories of heated petting sessions on abandoned bayou roads came instantly to mind. "There is one possibility. But I'll need to stop and make a call."

"Fine." That would give her time to gather up her composure and her nerve, both of which were beginning to disintegrate.

He pulled into the parking lot of a Piggly Wiggly and Bliss watched through the window as he made the brief call on the pay phone.

"All set," he said when he returned to the car. "So long as you're up for a little ride."

"It's a lovely evening for a ride." It was, indeed, a soft, pink evening, the air fresh from the light rain that had fallen while they'd been inside the plantation house, bidding against Churchill.

"How do you feel about boats?"

"I've never thought about them one way or the other. Why?"

"A friend of mine has a cabin in the bayou. He's not using it this weekend and said it's ours. If we want it." He tossed a small brown bag into the back seat. "It's stocked with food and basics and I picked up a couple of toothbrushes inside."

Bliss realized that during the nearly two weeks they'd spent together, she'd never seen him with anyone else but herself. And one other person.

"This friend wouldn't happen to be Michael, would it?"

"Actually, it is." He didn't mention that he, Michael and Roarke had all inherited equal shares in the cabin. He glanced over at her. "Would that bother you? His knowing that you're spending the night with me?"

"I don't know." Bliss thought about the idea. "I guess not. Besides," she said, her sense of humor returning to dispel her earlier uneasiness, "if you treat me badly, I can always get him to shoot you."

As he chuckled along with her, Shayne wondered what she'd say if she knew her words were not exactly an idle threat. Oh, Mike would never shoot him. However, there was always the chance that if he hurt Bliss too badly, he could end up as his big brother's punching bag.

"He said if we didn't call back to cancel, he'd call your grandmother for you. And feed the cat."

"That's very thoughtful of him."

"That's Mike, Mr. Thoughtful."

He didn't mention the warning that his brother had given him concerning Bliss's feelings. Not wanting to dwell on the negative, Shayne turned off onto a single-lane dirt road, and directed his atypically unsettled thoughts toward the night ahead.

THE AFTERNOON SUN was slanting low on the horizon, turning the dark waters to molten copper when Shayne stopped in front of a small dock. Tied up at the dock was a flat-bottomed boat.

Although she would have preferred something a bit more substantial, but trusting him implicitly, Bliss climbed into the boat. He started the engine with the same flair he appeared to do everything else and as they pulled away from the dock, Bliss was reminded of another boat ride she'd taken with this man and realized she'd begun to fall in love with him that first night.

They edged through the shallows, then skimmed across the water. "We're lucky," Shayne said over the drone of the motor, "the rains have raised the water. Sometimes the route turns to mud and you have to pole your way through, but we should have clear running."

"It sounds as if you've been here before."

"A few times," he hedged. "Mike used to use it as a hunting and fishing cabin."

It was that special, suspended time between day and night. The air was still, cicadas had begun to sing in the purple haze and fireflies were flitting through the limbs of moss-draped cypress. They came around a bend and suddenly the river opened onto what seemed to be a secret lake.

Located on the banks of the lake, beneath the limbs of a huge spreading oak tree hundreds of years old, was an old-style planters cabin set on stilts.

"This is it," Shayne said as he cut the engine. "It's not the Whitfield Palace, but at least it's private."

Not having known what to expect, but secretly fearing some ramshackle building that was on the verge of being reclaimed by the bayou, Bliss was more than a little relieved as she studied the cabin. Constructed of weather-bleached cypress, it boasted a screened front porch and an outside stairway to the *garçonnière*, that place beneath the roof that had originally been designed for the young men of large families to sleep. It appeared to have sprung naturally from the wetland surrounding it.

"It's lovely," she said. "And perfect for this place."

Until he felt the rush of cooling relief, Shayne hadn't

realized exactly how much her opinion mattered. As he helped her out of the boat, warning her to stay on the boards so she wouldn't step in the deep mud, he considered that he was on the verge of sinking into quicksand himself.

The strange thing was, although he'd always enjoyed his hit-and-run relationships with women no more eager to get involved than he, and though Bliss offered more complications than he needed in his life, Shayne couldn't have walked away even if he'd wanted to.

The inside of the cabin, while casually furnished, proved every bit as appealing as the outside. The pine furniture was obviously handmade, a black woodstove took up one corner of the main room, and in what she found to be a strangely appealing feminine touch for a hunting cabin, someone had hung moss green monk's cloth curtains on the screened windows.

"I can't see Mike doing that," Shayne said, when Bliss commented on the charm of the curtains. "It must have been that woman that Mike's brother's supposedly involved with."

"Daria Shea," Bliss said.

"You know her?"

"Everyone knows Daria. She's an assistant prosecutor who made a lot of headlines a few months ago when she nearly got herself killed investigating a group of prominent men who'd established a secret vengeance society. That's how Roarke met her. She's a nice woman."

"That's what Mike said."

There was a puzzling hint of disapproval in his tone Bliss couldn't quite decipher. "Have you ever met Roarke?"

"Yeah."

When he didn't elaborate, Bliss decided it was time to

mention the problem that had been nagging at her since she'd returned from Paris.

"Do you realize that you know just about everything about me? But I know nothing about you?"

Shayne froze. He'd been wondering when she was going to bring that up.

"That's not exactly true. I don't know everything about you. For instance, I don't know the name of the first guy who ever kissed you."

"Billy Roberts. We were in the second grade and he caught me on the school playground and wouldn't let me off the merry-go-round until I gave him a kiss."

"That doesn't count because it was coerced." Shayne rocked back on his heels and eyed the crackling flames with satisfaction. "The kid's lucky. These days he'd get arrested for sexual harassment. So, what was the first kiss you gave away willingly?"

"André Robicheaux. We were playing spin the bottle at a Mardi Gras party. I was madly in love with him all during high school."

"Lucky André. Ever wondered what happened to him?"

"He's married now with four kids. I'm godmother to his youngest daughter."

He thought about the kind of woman who could remain close friends with not only her first great love, but the man's wife, as well. This was yet more proof that he and Bliss were horrendously mismatched. She obviously savored old relationships the same way she favored antique furniture. Her roots ran deep in this hot, steamy land and he couldn't imagine her ever leaving.

While he, on the other hand, was a man incapable of settling down in one place, with one woman. Which made him just like his father. And just like Roarke had been, until he'd apparently fallen for a deputy prosecutor who sewed curtains.

Life had made him cynical, experience had made him unwilling to trust anyone, with the exception of his brothers. While Bliss, even after her debacle, trusted too easily.

"I suppose André was your first lover, then," he said.

"Actually, Alan was my first lover." She paused. "Which makes you my second."

Okay. Here was his cue, that nagging little voice of conscience told him. The only honorable thing to do would be to call this entire farce off now.

"If that's true, then all the men in New Orleans are either blind or out of their minds."

"Neither." She took a deep breath and met his eyes. "I was waiting until I met a man I felt I could love."

Love. The word came crashing down on him. "Bliss..." For once in his life, Shayne O'Malley, a man whose occupation demanded a glibness with words, could think of absolutely nothing to say.

"I'm sorry." She reached up and placed a palm on his cheek. "I wasn't going to say anything. At least not until...well, later." She hadn't wanted to risk frightening him away before she could experience the heights she suspected he'd bring to what with Alan had been a less than thrilling experience. "But what you told me earlier, about not being able to offer me forever, made me realize how much we're alike."

That was nearly as much a revelation as the fact that she loved him. "In what way?" Shayne managed to ask.

"We both respect the truth. No matter how painful it might prove to be. So, since you were so honest with me, I thought it only fair that I be equally as honest with you."

Hell. Shayne wondered if Roarke's old shotgun was still in the bedroom closet. It'd probably be easier to just shoot himself now, rather than wait until everything came crashing down around them. This warm-hearted, open woman deserved a much better man than he could ever be. If he lived a thousand lifetimes.

"I don't know what to say." Now that, at least, was the truth.

Her smile, echoed in her wide, expressive eyes, bathed him in a warmth like nothing he'd ever known. "You don't have to say anything, Shayne." She twined her fingers together around his neck. "Just make love to me. With me," she corrected, her voice trembling with a heady mixture of nerves and desire. "Please?"

He'd done his best to do the honorable thing. But reminding himself that he was only human, that he'd certainly never been bucking for sainthood—especially since Mike had already claimed that role in the O'Malley family by the time he'd been born—Shayne captured Bliss's silky soft, parted lips with his mouth, scooped her off her feet and carried her into the adjoining bedroom.

10

THE BED WAS soft, but not uncomfortably so. "It's like sinking into a cloud," Bliss murmured happily. "A lovely, fragrant cloud."

"It's stuffed with Spanish moss. And some herbs, but I don't know what kind."

"If the way I'm feeling is any indication, they're undoubtedly magical ones," she said as she reveled in the wondrous, mystical emotions being in this hidden, secret place with Shayne instilled.

The mattress rustled as he sat down beside her. "Believe me, sweetheart, I know the feeling." He touched his lips to hers and tasted her sigh. When he began slowly unbuttoning her blouse, she began to tremble.

Just as Shayne couldn't recall the last time he'd been with a woman capable of blushing, he couldn't remember ever being with one who trembled at his touch. The women he took to bed were experienced, worldly. Women who understood that seduction was, after all, merely an enjoyable game.

He folded the flowered silk back. She was wearing an ivory camisole trimmed with a delicate froth of lace. "You're so lovely."

Never had Bliss so wanted to believe a man. Never had she so wanted one to find her lovely. More than lovely, she thought as he touched his mouth to her collarbone and made her shiver.

She wanted to be stunning. Irresistible. She wanted to make him forget every other sophisticated woman he'd ever known. Women like that elegant blond she'd met in the bedroom in Paris, the kind of women who were born knowing how to wrap men around their bejeweled fingers.

"Are you afraid of me?" His lips smiled, although his eyes questioned.

"Not of you." The words clogged her throat as he skimmed a fingertip just above the lace, over the crest of her breasts. "Never of you." She hated the way her voice sounded so shaky. So needy. "It's just that I've never been very good at...well, I'm not really a physical person...I'm afraid I won't be able to give you what you want."

Vulnerability surrounded her like a shimmering aura, like the Saint Elmo's fire he'd witnessed innumerable times out here in the bayou. Never had Shayne been so humbled. And never, not even that first time, on a quilt in the bed of his brother Roarke's borrowed pickup truck, had Shayne been so nervous about doing this right.

"That's one thing you don't have to ever worry about, Bliss." He tamped down the desire to rip the rest of her clothes away and concentrated instead on the tenderness he was unaccustomed to feeling. "You have to trust me."

"I do." Her somber gaze echoed her whispered words. "Absolutely."

Such unqualified trust caused another sharp stab of guilt that Shayne steadfastly ignored. "Don't worry about giving," he murmured against her mouth. Her sweet, sweet mouth. "For now, just concentrate on taking."

The lingering kiss caused her head to spin, making it impossible for Bliss to argue, even if she'd wanted to. Which she definitely didn't.

He released her long enough to take off her shoes. Although she'd been tempted to wear heels to the auction—the better to show off her legs—in the end practicality had won out and she'd settled for a pair of petal pink ballet slipper styled flats.

She hadn't realized she'd been holding her breath as he'd unwound the satin ribbons crisscrossing her calves until he touched his lips to that startlingly sensitive spot behind her knee. The air came out of her lungs in a hot whoosh at the same time as she instinctively stiffened.

"Just relax," he crooned, caressing her lower leg in a way meant to soothe, rather than arouse. "It'll be all right. I'd never hurt you."

That, of course, was the lie of the millennium. He would hurt her; it had probably been unavoidable from the beginning. What was coming as a distinct surprise was Shayne's realization that he wasn't going to emerge from this assignment unscathed, either.

His hands moved over her shoulders, coaxing her muscles to relax, then down her arms. He linked their fingers together as his mouth returned to hers. The kiss that began with a snowflake soft touch gradually deepened, enticing her into the mists, exorcising her nervousness while steeping her in a warm, bone-melting pleasure.

"That's my Bliss." She felt his smile against her mouth. And then those teasing, talented lips were moving down her throat, warming her blood to a steamy temperature that rivaled a New Orleans summer afternoon. "You're so sweet." When he touched the tip of his tongue to the hollow at the base of her throat, she knew he could feel her pulse leap in response. "So soft." His mouth continued its quest, dampening the lace covering her breasts.

Her breathing slowed; although she still wanted him, more than ever, Bliss began to feel strangely languid as he proceeded to make love to her with his mouth alone.

Somehow—perhaps by magic?—he dispensed with the camisole. More relaxed than she'd ever been, she didn't feel the faintest bit self-conscious as he unbuttoned her flowered skirt and drew it slowly over her hips and down her bare legs.

He was so patient. So tender. He was, in every way, the man a little girl who'd believed in Prince Charming had spent so many lazy delta days daydreaming of. He was the man a young woman, so cruelly betrayed by the man she'd foolishly trusted, had come to believe did not exist.

But he did. Shayne Broussard was wonderfully, exquisitely real. And for the first time in her life, Bliss truly understood the term *making love.*

It had begun to rain. The sound of the raindrops on the tin roof overhead provided a musical counterpoint to the wind chimes outside the bedroom window and their shimmering sighs and soft moans.

Even as the building fire began to heat Bliss's flesh, Shayne refused to rush, taking his time, finding her innocent, instinctive responses amazingly arousing. What had ever made him think he preferred women of experience? he wondered as he touched his mouth to the silky skin beneath her breast and heard that husky sound of response deep in her throat.

When he nipped at the tender flesh of her inner thigh, heard her sharply drawn breath turn into a sultry laugh of delight as she experienced for the first time the thin line between pleasure and pain, suddenly, all the sexual gymnastics of his past life paled in comparison to what he realized, on some distant level, would prove to be a life-altering experience.

"I want..." Her hand floated up as if responding to a hypnotic suggestion. "I need..." Her lips, so thoroughly and wonderfully kissed, were too numb to form the words. Her mind was drifting on gilt-edged waves of pleasure she'd never suspected were possible.

"What is it, darlin'?" He caught her hand in midair and touched his open mouth to the inside of her wrist and imagined he could taste the hot, rapid bloodbeat. "Tell me what you want."

Words had always come so easily, so quickly. Until now. It was as if he'd stolen her capacity for speech along with her heart, Bliss thought as she took a deep breath and forced her floating mind to concentrate.

"I want to see you." She dreamily reached for him. "I want to touch you."

"I thought you'd never ask."

He brought her hand to his chest, forcing himself to remain patient while her fingers fumbled with the shirt buttons. But it was definitely worth the wait. When she finally freed him of the shirt, and pressed first her palms, then her lips against his chest, Shayne felt the jolt all the way through his aching loins.

"Dear Lord, I've tried to be patient," he groaned as he left the bed only long enough to rip off the rest of his clothes. "But I can't wait for you any longer."

The fire in his gaze surged through her body as Bliss looked up at this marvelously aroused male standing beside the bed. She'd done that, she thought dizzily, staring in wonder at the solid proof that he did, indeed, want her. The idea made her feel amazingly, wantonly, sexy.

"I don't want to wait any longer." She went up on her knees, wrapped her arms around his waist and pressed her mouth against the hot moist flesh of his stomach. "I think I've been waiting for this moment since Paris."

"That makes two of us." Shayne clung to control long enough to sheathe himself in the condom he'd bought in the grocery store earlier. Then, with a muffled sound that was part curse, part prayer, he dragged her down onto the bed and covered her soft, yielding body with his.

A pain stabbed through him as he entered her, first sharp, then unbearably sweet. Once again it crossed his mind that no woman had ever made him feel so real, so free, but before he could tell Bliss that this was different, that she was different, she'd wrapped her long legs around his hips and he began to move, slowly at first, then faster, harder, driving her deep into the fragrant moss-filled mattress, pushing them both closer and closer to the edge. And then beyond.

Afterward, lying in his arms, Bliss listened to the sound of the rain on the tin roof overhead and knew that she'd never hear rain again without thinking of Shayne. She'd never felt happier, more fulfilled, more loved. She wanted to tell him again that she loved him, but not wanting to scare him away, she contented herself with tracing her fingers through the dark arrow of hair that bisected his chest and listening to the beat of his heart beneath her cheek.

Shayne listened to the sound of the rain on the roof and knew that he'd never hear rain again without thinking of Bliss. It was not a happy thought. He'd never felt more miserable, more guilty, more angry at himself.

What had he been thinking of, allowing himself to lose control this way? What was she going to do when she found out the truth? Although it was already too late, he decided that it would be better to begin distancing himself now, before he made things even worse.

"I'm sorry," Bliss murmured as she felt him moving away.

Shayne immediately stiffened. She was sorry? "What on earth for?"

"I told you I wasn't very experienced." She lifted her head and met his strangely angry gaze. "But I've always been a quick learner, and—"

"Bliss, don't." Surrendering to the inevitable, he drew her against him and kissed her. A long, deep kiss meant to burn away any lingering insecurities she might be feeling. "It was wonderful," he said when they finally came up for air. "You were wonderful."

"Still, you're used to all those jet-set women..."

The kind her husband had preferred over her. She didn't say the words out loud, but Shayne got the meaning, loud and clear.

"Are you asking for a comparison? As if I keep some sort of mental scorecard? Or perhaps even a little black book where I rate women from one to ten?"

Feeling horribly foolish, Bliss wished she hadn't even brought the subject up. "Never mind." She began searching through the tangled sheets for her clothes. Where on earth was her underwear? Talking about sex was difficult enough without having to do it stark naked.

"It's not important." She managed to find her panties, the ones with the little ribbons that Shayne had seemed to enjoy untying.

"Of course it is." He snatched the minuscule piece of

silk out of her hand and tossed it aside. "It's important because you're important, Bliss."

"I wasn't fishing for compliments."

When she turned away, he caught her chin between his thumb and forefinger and turned her head back toward him. "If I had a little black book, which I don't, you'd rate at least an eleven which would put you way above the pack, if there was any comparison, but there's not.

"Sex is easy, Bliss. Too easy, sometimes." He felt somewhat uncomfortable about all the willing women he'd tangled the sheets with over the years. "But after a while, if you manage to keep emotions from getting involved, it becomes too much like plumbing...what fits where. And it starts to lose its appeal.

"I don't want to think about Alan Fortune when I'm in bed with you, so I'm going to say this once, then I don't want to talk about the bastard again. If he was too stupid to realize what a gem he had in you, then it was his loss. If he was too self-centered to take time to show you what pleasure two people can share, then he's a fool. And if things weren't what they should have been between the two of you in bed, did you ever stop to think that it was his fault? And not yours?"

No. That thought, amazingly, had never crossed her mind. "But all those women—"

"Dammit!" He dragged his fingers through his hair and wondered how the hell they'd gotten off onto this track. At least he wasn't feeling guilty anymore. What he was feeling was angry. And frustrated. "I told you, it's easy to find women to go to bed with. What's difficult is finding that one-in-a-million woman who can make it special."

And remarkably, she was that woman, Bliss reminded

herself. Shayne had shown her with every touch, every kiss. She'd just been too insecure to realize what he'd been telling her.

"You're right."

"Of course I am." The anger drained out of him, replaced by a tenderness that was far more dangerous.

"There is just one little thing." She twined her arms around his neck.

"What's that?" He kissed her lips, lightly, lovingly.

"Even if you're right about me being special—"

"You are." Although it muddied the waters even further, it was one of the few absolute truths Shayne was able to tell her.

"Thank you." She dimpled prettily. "However, the truth is that despite the fact that I was married, I'm still pretty inexperienced at all this. So, I was thinking..."

She ran her hands enticingly down his chest, over his stomach, then lower still. Her fingers circled his sex, which stirred beneath her stroking touch.

"You were thinking?" he managed to whisper as he felt the blood leaving his head again, rushing down to more vital organs.

"Well, you know what they say about practice making perfect."

He laughed at that, a rich explosion of sound that expunged the last of the lingering tension between them. "Darlin', I'm all yours."

And the wonderful thing was, Bliss thought, as she pushed him back onto the mattress and began treating him to the same tender torment he'd subjected her to, it was true.

"WE NEED TO TALK."

Night had fallen. They were sitting at the table, soup

heating on the stove, Bliss perched on Shayne's lap. He stroked her back, enjoying the sensual feel of warm silk beneath his fingertips.

"Mmm." She touched her mouth to his. "I love talking with you. I love it when you tell me how beautiful I am." The tip of her tongue touched the notch between lips she'd decided were as beautifully formed as any statue created by Renaissance sculptors. "How hot I am." Her words were punctuated with short kisses. "How much you want me."

"Bliss…" Amazingly, after all they'd shared, her generous mouth, her breathy voice, her closeness, all served to make him want her all over again. Knowing it was the honorable, the only thing to do, Shayne tried yet again to explain the events that had brought him into her life. "This is serious."

She drew her head back and studied him. "It also sounds unpleasant."

"I suppose that depends on your point of view," he hedged. "It's about Alan and—"

"You're the one who didn't want to bring Alan into this wonderful place. And you're right. So, I'm not going to discuss him with you, Shayne. Not now. And not here."

"It's important."

"I understand that." She put her hands on his shoulders. "And I realize that whatever is happening to us isn't happening in a vacuum. We both come with past experiences, other people in our lives.

"However, since I can't remember ever being this happy, I'm not going to allow anything to ruin this one perfect night."

Even though he'd wanted to clear the air, Shayne told

himself that since he'd been lying to her for weeks, what difference would one more night make?

"Far be it from me to ruin perfection."

"That's better." She rewarded him with a longer kiss that promised future delights. Her mouth, which had been as serious as her gaze, tilted into a softly enticing smile he found impossible to resist. "And now that we've gotten that settled, I have a request."

"Anything," he said promptly, meaning it.

"Ever since I saw that wonderful fur rug, I've been fantasizing about making love on it."

She hadn't been alone. "I think that sounds terrific." He stood up, holding her in his arms as he walked the few feet to the rug. "However, I'd think it was just as terrific making love to you on a bed of stones."

She laughed as he laid her on the soft black fur, her voice reminding him of the wind chimes someone—undoubtedly Daria—had hung outside the bedroom window. "The way we're going, we may get to that yet."

THEIR MAGICAL, STOLEN time together passed all too soon. The following day, Bliss sighed as Shayne pulled the boat up to the dock.

"I hate leaving paradise to return to earth and the real world."

"We'll come back," Shayne promised, conveniently overlooking the fact that once he got this case settled he'd be on his way. To some other intrigue, another city, another woman.

When that idea failed to prove even slightly appealing, he realized that Bliss Fortune had done more than get under his skin. She had him by the throat. In a stranglehold.

But even that power, which he suspected she didn't

even realize she possessed, would not be enough to keep her from getting hurt. He should leave, Shayne thought grimly. He should just turn the damn case over to Cunningham and get out now, while he still could.

It's what his father would have done. Roarke, too, before he'd gotten himself tied up in pretty ribbons with a smart, apparently gutsy woman who sewed curtains and enjoyed making love to the sound of music made by the wind chimes.

Bliss had talked all the way back in the boat, already reminiscing about their short time together, the memories that would have to last them both a lifetime. He'd marveled at her eye for detail; he doubted that a single star or streak of gilded sunrise had escaped her attention. She seemed to find wonder in everything, from the graceful blue herons to the furry fat nutria they'd found sunning themselves in front of the cabin to the pebbly-backed alligators carrying their young on their back.

But now, obviously sensitive to his turmoiled, half-angry emotions, she'd fallen uncharacteristically silent. Which made him feel guiltier than ever.

"I have something for you," he said as they reached the car. "Sort of a gift."

"I love presents."

"It's nothing all that much." Having already determined that her love for antiques echoed old-fashioned beliefs, he suspected that after last night, she'd be hoping for a ring.

"I mean, it's not all that expensive, and I just bought it on a whim, because I thought you'd enjoy it, but—"

"Shayne." She touched her fingertips to his lips. "I'd treasure anything you gave me. Honest."

Honest. That damn word just kept cropping up over and over again, underlying why this relationship would never—could never—work. Although he'd managed to halfway convince himself that his motives were pure, the bottom line was that he'd proven no better than her lying, cheating slime of an ex-husband.

He cursed silently as he opened the trunk, calling himself all the unflattering names he suspected she'd fling at him when she discovered the truth. He took the box out and practically shoved it into her arms.

She looked with puzzlement at the familiar wrapping. "This is from my shop."

"I know." His nerves were screeching. He couldn't remember when he'd been so tense giving a woman a simple gift. Then again, Shayne reminded himself, there was nothing simple about either Bliss or his feelings for her. And that, apparently, made all the difference. "Would you just open it?"

Surprise at his gruff tone registered on her face, but she did as he asked.

"Oh, Shayne." It was a whisper, shimmering like the pink-tinged early morning fog that had surrounded the cabin while they'd made slow, magical love on the lush fur rug. Tears glistened wetly in her eyes. "It's Raggedy Ann."

"It was silly, I know, but—"

"Not at all." It was his turn to put his hand to her mouth, forestalling her words. "I was watching you wrap her up for that German tourist. Even though I didn't know the whole story at the time, I could see you didn't want to let her go.

"Now that I've heard about your childhood, with your mother's drinking problem and the difficulties at school, I suspect Raggedy Ann meant a lot more to you than a mere doll and I'm glad I was able to get her back for you."

"She was a good listener." Bliss stroked the curly red yarn hair that had soaked up so many salty tears over the years. "But I'm grown up now, and it was such a tight month, trying to pay the bills before the things from the Paris trip earned back their investment, I thought I might as well pick up enough to pay the phone bill." Her teary smile tore at something elemental deep inside Shayne. "I missed her the minute I watched her leave the shop."

"I know." He forced a smile he was a very long way from feeling. "A bit of advice, darlin'. If you ever decide to pay a visit to any of the casinos, don't play poker. Because every thought you have gets written across your face in neon letters a mile high."

She managed a shaky laugh. "Zelda always said the same thing when I was trying to avoid getting punished when I was a little girl. Good thing I didn't decide to grow up and become a con artist. Or a spy."

Both those descriptions hit a little too close to home for comfort. "Good thing," Shayne agreed.

She put the doll down onto the closed trunk, wrapped her arms around his waist, and pressed her cheek against his chest. "Thank you, Shayne," she murmured into his shirt. "You couldn't have given me a more wonderful gift. Diamonds, emeralds, Tiffany's entire stock, couldn't equal what this means to me. I'll remember it always."

Shayne suspected that was unfortunately true. And that when the unpalatable truth came out, she'd never forget—or forgive—him.

Unaccustomed to experiencing such wrenching emotions, and not knowing how to extricate himself from this sticky web of deception and intrigue he'd spun,

Shayne found himself suddenly engulfed in a tidal wave of fear, frustration and fury.

Acting solely on instinct, he tangled his hands in the fiery silk of her hair, lifted her head and crushed his mouth to hers.

Bliss tried not to be uncomfortable by the way Shayne hardly said two words to her during the drive back to New Orleans. The part of her that remained an unrelenting optimist was sure his silence was only his way of dealing with the changes in their relationship. She suspected he'd felt things he hadn't expected to feel.

And so had she. Heavens, what she'd felt, she mused, arching her back and stretching her legs in an attempt to work out kinks and faint aches earned during a night of vigorous exercise. Just the memory of all the things they'd done made her blush. And smile.

Bliss wasn't as disturbed as she might have been that Shayne still hadn't shared any real details of his past life with her. After all, she'd been the one who'd placed that moratorium on talking during their stolen interlude. Besides, even without words, he'd opened himself up to her, revealing a tender, sensitive side that was a marked contrast to his usual suave masculine confidence.

It would be all right, Bliss assured herself. Shayne Broussard might not realize it himself yet, but she knew, without a single doubt, that he was falling in love with her. As she had with him.

She held the idea close to her heart, where it warmed and comforted her.

Dammit, Shayne thought grumpily, didn't she know what she was doing to him? The woman flat out didn't fight fair. Here he was, trying to figure out ways to get out of this mess with as few hurt feelings as possible, and she had to start moving around that way.

Did she know that when she arched her back, like some sleek Siamese cat, that it made her breasts stick out in a way that made him ache to take them in his mouth? Did she realize that when she stretched her long firm legs out, it reminded him in vivid detail exactly how they'd felt wrapped around his hips as he'd driven her deeper and deeper into the Spanish moss-stuffed mattress?

Did she know she was driving him out of his freaking mind?

Of course she did, Shayne decided.

"You keep wiggling around like that, sugar," he warned, "and I'm going to pull over and take you right here alongside the road in the bright morning sunlight."

The smile she flashed him was hot, sultry and sexy as hell. "Promises, promises," she all but purred.

Hell. Shayne curled his fingers more tightly around the steering wheel as he realized somehow, when he wasn't looking during the long love-filled night, he'd lost all control of the situation.

"IF YOU DON'T MIND," Bliss said later, as they crossed the bridge into the city, "I'd like to stop by the shop before dinner."

"Sure."

His voice was rough and curt, almost annoyed. Bliss wished that this wasn't so difficult for him. That he could feel even a portion of what she was feeling.

He had in the cabin. She'd sensed him relaxing that strange vigilance she'd noticed about him from the beginning, watched him open himself up to the emotions—and the love—they'd shared. The memory had her wondering about her chances of keeping Shayne in bed twenty-four hours a day, which led to another idle fantasy of chaining him to the lovely wrought iron head-board she'd bought at an estate sale in Savannah, until he saw the light.

"You know, if you don't want to come to dinner, Zelda will understand—"

"I told you I would."

She shrugged. "Fine."

Terrific. Now he'd gone and hurt her feelings. As he turned onto Magazine Street, Shayne despised himself.

"What in the world?"

Bliss stared in wonder at the phalanx of black-and-white squad cars parked in front of The Treasure Trove. The bubble lights on the tops of a few of the cars were still flashing red and blue. Spectators lined the sidewalk on either side of the bright yellow police tape.

Shayne cursed. Obviously Cunningham had gotten tired of waiting for him to unearth the jewels and taken matters into his own clumsy hands.

"You must have had a break-in." He hoped that was all it was, but was afraid it was a great deal more than that.

"A break-in in broad daylight?" she questioned, as if reading his mind. "Oh, my God." Her hand flew to her mouth, her eyes widened with fear. "They wouldn't send this many police for a break-in. If Lilah was hurt, I'll never forgive myself."

"Let's not jump to conclusions," Shayne said, trying to calm her down. But she was out of the car, running across the street before he could finish. He cursed again, hotly, parked the car and took off after her.

11

SHAYNE HAD NEVER been so happy to see his brother as he was when he saw Michael grab hold of Bliss, stopping her from going into the shop. As Shayne dodged a taxi, barely missing ending up on the hood, he watched the two of them struggling. Despite her obvious determination, given Mike's size, it wasn't any contest.

"What happened?" Shayne asked his brother.

Before Michael could answer, a man wearing a rain-rumpled suit came up to them. "Ms. Fortune?" He held up a badge in a small leather shield. "I'm Detective Mark Roberts, from the homicide squad, and—"

"Homicide? Is my assistant..." She swallowed. "Is Lilah..." She couldn't say the word.

"Ms. Middleton is going to be fine," the detective assured her. "She was checked out by a doctor on the scene, then sent home."

"Then it was a robbery?"

Relieved that Lilah had survived without harm, Bliss tried to remember the deductible on her insurance and realized that her mind had gone totally blank. She knew that New Orleans's police force, like that of so many other cities, was suffering a shortage, but surely it wasn't standard practice to assign homicide detectives to a common robbery?

"The inside's been ransacked pretty badly, so we're having a little trouble deciding about that, which is where you can help us. But I'm afraid we're also dealing with a murder here, Ms. Fortune."

"A murder?" She didn't understand. If Lilah was all right, and Michael was standing here on the sidewalk with her, who could have been in her store?

"It was Alan, Bliss," Michael said quietly.

"Alan?" She stared up at him. "Alan killed someone?" She couldn't imagine such a thing. He might be a rat and a scoundrel, but his weapon of choice had always been charm.

"Alan's the one who was killed," Michael revealed.

"Alan's dead?" That was more impossible to accept than the idea of her former husband killing someone.

"He was shot in the head at close range," Detective Roberts said. "I'm afraid I'm going to have to ask you, Ms. Fortune, where you were between midnight and when Ms. Middleton opened the shop at ten o'clock this morning."

"She was with me," Shayne said. "We spent the night away from the city."

"And you are?"

Knowing that the ruse was up, Shayne exchanged a brief look with Michael. "My name's Shayne," he said slowly. "Shayne O'Malley."

Even as he said the fateful words, Shayne knew that if he was unfortunate enough to live to be a hundred, he'd never forget the sound of Bliss's pained gasp. Or the bleak betrayal in her soft innocent eyes.

"You don't understand," Bliss said two hours later, after the police had finished questioning her and they'd taken Alan's body away. She knew that the horrifying image of her lifeless ex-husband would remain with her for a very long time. "I don't want to talk to you, Shayne.

We've nothing to say to one another." She held tightly to Hercules. Bliss had been relieved to discover the cat hiding behind a cabinet.

"That's not true," he argued. "You know you want to call me every name in the book, and believe me, sweetheart—"

"Don't call me sweetheart!"

"All right." He lifted his hands in a gesture of surrender.

Folding her arms over her chest in an unconscious gesture of self-protection, she turned away from the man who'd betrayed her so horribly, the man she'd been foolish enough to fall in love with. When her gaze settled on that dark spot on the floor where Alan's head had lain, little white dots began to swim in front of her eyes.

Seeing the color fade from her face, Shayne caught her by the shoulders. "Sit down." He literally pushed her and the cat into a nearby Windsor rocking chair. "Put your head between your knees."

"Don't touch me!" She tried for hauteur and outrage, but the vertigo was winning.

"It'll help, Bliss," Michael, who'd vouched for Shayne, then stayed after the police had left, advised quietly. "You need to get the blood back into your head or you'll faint."

"I don't want to talk to you, either," she insisted. Nevertheless she did as both brothers instructed. Bliss didn't know whether to be relieved or more angry when their advice worked. "You're as bad as Shayne. Worse," she told him, "since I thought we were friends."

"We were. Are," Michael corrected.

"But blood's thicker than water, right?" When he didn't answer, she risked raising her head, relieved that the blizzard of spots had dwindled to a flurry. "Given a choice between your friend or your brother, you had no choice but to side with your brother, right? Even if the brother in question is a liar."

"It was more complicated than that, dammit."

Bliss was about to answer when the door to The Treasure Trove suddenly opened and Hercules hissed at the newcomer.

"Good afternoon, Ms. Fortune," Cunningham greeted her politely. "I believe it's time we met."

Bliss's gaze was wary. Her fingers tightened on the orange fur. "Who are you?"

"I'm Agent Cunningham." He wisked a folder out of the pocket of his suit jacket, and revealed a badge a lot like the one the detective had shown her, but with an insignia Bliss didn't recognize. "I'm Shayne O'Malley's superior. And the man who assigned him to make the initial contact with you in Paris."

"Assigned?" Her head whipped from Cunningham to Shayne. "I was nothing but an assignment all along?"

She'd believed, after surviving the damage that Alan had done to her heart, that she'd emerged so strong that no one would ever be able to hurt her again. Obviously, Bliss thought now, she'd been wrong. Dead wrong.

"I told you," Shayne insisted, "we need to talk."

If her mind hadn't been whirling, if she hadn't been so shattered, Bliss would have heard the stress and pain in his voice. But at the moment, all she could concentrate on was the depth of his betrayal.

"And I told you, we have nothing to talk about."

"I'm afraid that's where you're mistaken." Cunningham's tone was as smooth and deadly as a stiletto. "We have a great deal to discuss with you, Ms. Fortune."

He settled down in a Queen Anne chair facing the rocker. "Now, we can do this one of two ways. We can have a nice, friendly discussion here in your lovely little shop. Or I can have you taken downtown to the police station, where I'm afraid the atmosphere is far less appealing."

Personally, Bliss found nothing appealing about that ugly blood stain darkening the plank floor. Or the lingering aura of death she could feel hovering over the room. On the other hand, the alternative was also not at all attractive.

"Michael?" Conveniently forgetting she'd vowed never speak to him again, she turned toward the man who she could at least trust to tell her the truth about her rights. "Can he do that?"

"I'm afraid so, honey. But you've the right to an attorney—"

"An attorney? Why would I need a lawyer? Detective Roberts said I wasn't a suspect—"

"Not in the murder," Shayne interrupted. He'd always meant to tell her. Just not this way. "All personal problems aside, one of the reasons I needed to talk with you—hopefully before Cunningham showed up—is because the government believes you're somehow involved with an international jewel smuggling ring."

"What?" The blizzard was back, blinding in its intensity. Refusing to surrender to it in front of Shayne and his superior, Bliss blinked furiously, willing her head to clear.

"Actually," Cunningham revealed, "you were considered, for a time, the ringleader."

"A jewel thief?" Bliss stared at Shayne. There couldn't possibly be any more. "You thought I was a jewel thief?"

He raked his fingers through his dark hair and shot Cunningham a killing look. He'd never seen an interview handled with less finesse.

"In the beginning, perhaps, but—"

"And you, Michael?" Cutting Shayne off, she turned to his brother. "Did you believe I was a thief?"

"Not for a minute," Michael answered without hesitation. "And, I know I'm standing on thin ice here when it comes to credibility, but Shayne eventually realized that the government was barking up the wrong tree, too."

"Oh?" Her tone was more glacial than either man had ever heard it. As Shayne watched, she encased herself in enough ice to cover Jupiter several times over. "Was this before or after you slept with me?"

"Dammit, Bliss, if you'd just listen—"

"Perhaps you two can settle whatever personal problems you have later," Cunningham suggested silkily. "Right now, I'd like to get this case wrapped up. Which it seems we're going to be able to do, now that it's obvious that Fortune was the guilty one all along."

Alan a jewel thief. That wasn't an impossible stretch, Bliss realized. After all, she'd been the one who'd sarcastically accused him of having probably stolen a Fabergé egg.

"I still don't understand what all this has to do with me," she complained.

"It would be my guess that he's been using your antique shop as a drop-off point for stolen merchandise for some time."

"That's impossible!" Bliss jumped to her feet. Hercules meowed a complaint, then deftly jumped to his perch in the sun-filled window. "Until we ran into each other in Paris, I haven't seen him since our divorce."

"You wouldn't have had to have been directly involved," Cunningham said. "He could have easily paid off one of the dealers you work with to include the stolen jewels in a shipment. Then, when the item in question went on sale, he could have had an associate come in and buy it."

Even as she opened her mouth to say that was an outlandish scenario, Bliss remembered Alan's insistence that she must give back the necklace. At the time she'd been too distracted by his behavior to pay enough attention, but it seemed he'd mentioned something about a recent shipment.

"I suppose you'll want the list of things I bought in Paris. And where I bought them," she murmured, rubbing her temple where a killer headache was pounding.

"O'Malley already took care of that," Cunningham informed her.

Bliss shot a killing glare at Shayne, whose face had returned to its characteristically inscrutable expression. The least he could do was squirm a little, she thought with a burst of irritation.

"Agent O'Malley appears quite efficient."

"He's one of our best," Cunningham agreed. "Although his methods tend to be unconventional, he usually achieves results."

"How nice to know my tax dollars aren't being wasted." Icicles dripped from every word as Bliss wondered how many suspects he'd taken to bed over the years. Something suddenly occured to her.

"Whose house was I supposed to be decorating?"

"The government's," Cunningham said. "It's a safe house. We've used it for debriefing former spies, drug dealers, federal informants."

"How did you do that without any furniture?" she asked. Then comprehension dawned. "Agent O'Malley had it all moved out."

"I told you his methods are often unconventional.

And expensive." It was Cunningham's turn to glare at Shayne. "I just received the bill for yesterday's little shopping spree."

Shayne shrugged. "I did what it took to keep the ball in play."

Including sleeping with her? Bliss wondered as her head pounded with increased force. Try as she might, she couldn't completely accept that what she and Shayne had shared last night and this morning had meant nothing to him. She wanted—needed—to believe that at least a part of his heart had been involved.

But in order to find out, she'd have to ask him directly, which she couldn't do with Cunningham and Michael here. And there was no way she ever intended to be alone with him again.

Turning down Michael's suggestion that she call her attorney, she spent the next three hours going through her appointment calendar and a year of purchase orders, and was not at all pleased to discover how often she'd received a shipment from France or Great Britain shortly after a major jewel theft.

"That's why you were a suspect," Cunningham told her. "To tell you the truth, we'd begun to believe that you and your former husband were in business together."

"We were divorced," she returned, closing her eyes as the image of Alan's dead body swam in her mind again. She'd fantasized about his death innumerable times, but she'd never actually meant for such a thing to happen.

"Greed is a powerful motive," Cunningham answered. "It made sense that just because you weren't willing to put up with the guy's infidelity didn't mean you weren't willing to make whatever untaxable money you could by being part of his illegal schemes."

Her head cleared again, the mental image of her ex-spouse blown away by the fresh breeze of renewed irritation. "You obviously don't know me very well."

"Not as well as O'Malley does." His smile was rife with sexual innuendo that made her fingers itch to slap him. She could feel Shayne's intense gaze but steadfastly refused to look at him.

"Shut up, Cunningham," Shayne growled softly.

"Be that as it may," she said, continuing to ignore Shayne, "if you've been investigating me all this time, you should know that my grandmother and I don't live a luxurious life-style. Almost every penny I make goes right back into the shop."

"Offshore banks exist for hiding illegal funds."

"But you could never find an account for me."

"No."

She sat back in the chair, rocking slowly as she thought about everything Cunningham had said. "I have one question."

"What's that?"

"If you truly believed that I was capable of such criminal activities, why aren't I a suspect in Alan's death?"

"Because you were with O'Malley."

"Ah, but did you ever think that he was just an alibi? That I'd arranged to spend the night away from the city, then lured Alan to The Treasure Trove, and had a hired killer—a hit man, I believe he's called—murder him?"

"Bliss," Michael warned quietly, "I don't think you should be talking like this without an attorney."

"Why not?" She turned toward him, her smile bright and horribly false. "Just think, Michael, you're the only man I know who routinely carries a gun. Perhaps you're the killer I hired. It makes a nice ironic touch, don't you think? My being so clever to pit the O'Malley brothers against each other in my little murder scheme?

"Oh, but there's just one flaw in that theory," she continued. "I would have had to know that Shayne was your brother. And of course I had no way of knowing that since the man I knew as Shayne Broussard was such an excellent liar."

"It wasn't all lies, Bliss," Shayne said quietly.

She ignored him. "Is this going to take much longer?" she asked, turning toward Cunningham. "Because I really would like to get home. I'm sure Zelda must be frantic by now."

"I called her and explained what was happening," Michael said. "I also called Dr. Vandergrift and asked him to drop by and make certain she was doing all right."

"Aren't you a dear, considerate friend," Bliss drawled, the hardness in her eyes at odds with the sweet syrup coating her words.

Michael met her scathing gaze head-on. "I try."

The thing Bliss found most irritating was both O'Malley brothers' refusal to crawl. Although each had admitted to having done wrong, they still possessed that steely core of self-confidence that made her want to start throwing things at them.

Now that she knew the truth, she realized that she'd been right to keep comparing the two men. Along with their physical resemblance, they were remarkably alike. Which, of course, made this entire episode even more confusing and unsettling.

She'd always considered Michael an unfailingly honest man, willing to give up a career he'd loved rather than compromise his integrity.

Shayne, on the other hand, was an unscrupulous liar

who'd say anything, do anything, to achieve what he wanted. To him, apparently, the ends truly did justify the means.

How could they be so much alike, when their differences were like night and day? The question made her headache pound even harder.

Cunningham capped his Waterman pen and put it back into his jacket pocket. "I believe that's enough for now, Ms. Fortune," he said. "From all the evidence O'Malley's compiled on you, I have to say that you don't fit the profile for a jewel thief. Or a murderer. I'm certain that when I turn in my report, my own superiors will mark your part of the case closed."

"Isn't that a relief." Although her tone was sarcastic, Bliss truly was relieved to discover that this might actually be the end of her nightmare. "I suppose I should consider myself fortunate that Agent O'Malley is such an excellent undercover officer."

She stood up. "If you gentlemen will excuse me, I have some cleaning up to do."

"Not today." Risking her wrath, Shayne took hold of the tops of both her arms. "You've been through too much. You need to let me take you home and—"

"Let go of me, Shayne. Right now."

"Not until we—"

"Shayne." Michael put his hand on his brother's shoulder. "Let me try." He turned toward Bliss. "I know you'd rather hang out with a gator right now than give me the time of day, but I don't really care how angry you are, Bliss. Because Shayne's right. You've received a couple of knockdown punches and you need to get out of here.

"Besides," he said, when she opened her mouth to argue, "Zelda was close to frantic when she heard about a body being found in the store. She was so afraid it was you, and even after I managed to assure her that you were safe, it took all my persuasive powers to keep her from racing down here.

"You need to go home. And your grandmother needs you there."

"Dammit, Michael," Bliss said, blinking back the traitorous tears threatening at the back of her eyelids, "I really, really want to dislike you."

"I know." He touched his fingertips to her temple, as if to soothe the pain he knew must be throbbing beneath the skin. "And if you want to call me every name in the book while I drive you home, that's okay. You won't think of any I haven't already been called. After all those years on the force, I've developed a pretty thick skin.

"But let me drive you home, so you can take care of Zelda. And she can take care of you."

He seemed to be the same warm, considerate man she'd come to care for so deeply. Since she also knew that loyalty ran deep in his veins, Bliss realized exactly how difficult a situation Shayne had put his older brother in.

That idea helped focus her anger on Shayne while allowing Michael to help her, since in truth, now that the initial shock was over, she was beginning to tremble so badly she wasn't certain she'd be able to drive herself home.

"On one condition," she said.

"You name it," Michael answered promptly.

"One word about your brother and I'm going to get out of the car and walk home."

"It's a deal." He gave her the first smile she'd seen since she'd arrived at The Treasure Trove, then handed her his car keys. "The car's parked right next door. Why don't you go sit in it while I lock up here?"

She glanced around the shop, her gaze settling on the dark stain once again. "Thank you." She took the keys, scooped Hercules from the window, then walked on wobbly legs out the door.

Shayne caught up with her on the sidewalk.

"I don't want you to touch me," she snapped as he put his arm around her waist.

"Tough. Because you look about ready to fall on your face." He took the keys from her nerveless fingers, dispatched the car alarm and opened the passenger door. "Get in."

"I don't have to take orders from you."

"It's not an order. It's a damn suggestion."

"I'm not talking to you." Since she was afraid she was going to embarrass herself by fainting, she slid into the bucket seat.

"Fine. Then if you'll just listen—"

"I'm not listening, either." She was tempted to put her hands on her ears, but deciding that would look horrendously juvenile, just stared straight ahead out the front windshield instead.

He leaned into the car. "I know I hurt you, Bliss. And I'm willing to plead guilty. But with an explanation, if you'll only hear it."

She snatched the keys from his hand, stuck them in the ignition, and twisted them to allow her to turn on the radio, which was tuned to an oldies rock station. Jim Croce was singing "Time in a Bottle."

Terrific timing, Bliss mused miserably. Had it only been a few hours ago that she'd been wishing she could freeze time so she'd never have to lose the joy she'd felt after her wonderous, stolen night with Shayne?

"Dammit, Bliss—"

She turned the volume up, drowning him out.

"All right." He shouted to be heard over the radio. "I'll leave you alone for now. But believe me, lady, this isn't over. Not by a long shot."

Frustrated, he grabbed hold of her chin and jerked her head toward him and gave her a quick hard angry kiss that was nothing like the sweet slow ones they'd shared this morning.

"It's not over," he repeated gruffly when he released her mouth. "That was just to keep you from forgetting what we have."

As if she could ever forget. Bliss watched as Shayne strode back to the shop and paused beside his brother who was locking the front door. Although she could see his lips move, she couldn't discern what he was saying.

"Take care of her," Shayne instructed Michael. "She needs more than a friend right now. She needs a protector."

Michael cut a quick glance toward Bliss, then back to his brother. "You're thinking the same thing I am."

"Yeah." Shayne rubbed the back of his neck, where the muscles had twisted into a painful knot. "Whoever killed Alan is still out there. And she's a potential target."

"I'll put one of my men at her house. Then I'll get back to digging into who the guy's been hanging out with lately."

"Thanks." Shayne wanted to hug his big brother, something that had been so easy to do back when he was six and Mike had gotten his kite out of a tree or untangled a fishing line. "I'm sorry I got you into this mess."

"Didn't anyone ever tell you? That's what big brothers are for."

"I'm serious," Shayne said. "If you ever need my help—"

"You'll be the first I call. If I can find you, that is."

Shayne turned to look over at Bliss, who appeared so small and pale in the front seat of Michael's car. "I think that's going to be a lot easier in the future."

"Thinking of sticking around?"

"A guy gets a little tired of living in hotels."

"Yeah, that's the same thing Roarke said. Right before he moved in with Daria."

"This is different." No way was Shayne going to start letting Bliss measure for curtains. But neither was he going to let her get away. Not until this fever between them had run its course.

"Of course it is," Michael said with a laugh that suggested he didn't believe his brother for a minute. "I'll come by the hotel after I get Bliss settled in at home. And we'll see what we can come up with."

The two brothers parted; Michael headed off to Bliss, and Shayne returned to where he'd illegally parked in a yellow zone across the street. He plucked the ticket from the windshield wiper, stuck it into the glove compartment with the others he'd collected during his time in the city, then drove to the hotel. It was time, he decided, that he and Cunningham had a heart-to-heart talk.

12

"I DON'T KNOW what you're talking about." Cunningham's expression was as smooth as glass. But Shayne suspected he knew a lot more about Alan Fortune's death than he was saying. "If you're suggesting that I had anything to do with Fortune's untimely demise—"

"I'm suggesting you had someone take him out."

"And what would I achieve by killing the man?" Cunningham countered. "If he was involved in the jewel theft ring, and it appears that he indeed was, he would have been a great deal more help to us alive. Dead men can't talk," he reminded Shayne.

Shayne reluctantly agreed his superior had a point. Still, there'd been something niggling at the back of his mind for the past two days. Some piece of the puzzle he couldn't quite get his hands on.

"Which is why he was killed," Shayne surmised. "To keep him quiet."

"That would be my guess."

"The killer could have been a professional hit man who's already blown town." Shayne began to pace, trying to work out the logistics. But it was difficult when images of Bliss's face after she'd learned his true identity kept floating to the forefront of his mind. "Or, it could be someone local."

"Who knew both Fortunes," Cunningham agreed.

"Exactly. Which narrows things down to the grandmother. Or Nigel Churchill." Zelda, of course, was ridiculous. But the antique dealer suddenly moved higher on Shayne's suspect list.

"I wasn't aware that Churchill and Fortune were acquainted."

"They're old friends. In fact, Bliss told me Fortune introduced her to Churchill in the first place." Shayne stood in front of the window, looking down on the Quarter, which harbored a lot more dangerous secrets than tourists, who tended to focus on the jazz and strip clubs, could ever imagine.

New Orleans was as layered and multifaceted as its residents, and although it put on a carefree face for visitors, Shayne knew that it also had a darker side it kept to itself. In that respect, Shayne figured, he was a great deal like his hometown.

"The problem is, if Churchill was involved in the jewelry smuggling, why wouldn't he move stuff through his own shops?" Shayne mused out loud.

"Perhaps it was too dangerous," Cunningham suggested. "Since he's been trying to take over the Fortune woman's business, it would only make sense that he'd keep track of her trips abroad. It wouldn't be that difficult to arrange to have the merchandise smuggled in her purchases."

"That way, if the stuff got caught at customs, Bliss would be the one holding the bag." It made sense, Shayne decided. "But that's awfully iffy. What if someone actually bought the item in question before the contact on this end could get hold of it?"

"That would make things more difficult," Cunningham allowed.

"It's too risky," Shayne muttered.

"If thieves and foreign agents didn't make mistakes, we'd never catch them."

"Good point."

Once again Shayne had the feeling that there was something not quite right with the scenario. Something that didn't ring true. But he couldn't put his finger on it.

"At least Bliss is off the hook."

"I'm afraid I have to agree with you."

Shayne lifted a brow. "Afraid?"

"It would have been a great deal more convenient if she had been the thief. We'd have closed this case by now and moved on."

As they always did. Usually, by the time a case was closed Shayne was more than ready to move on to the next one. But that wasn't true this time, and although he'd been fighting it from the beginning, he knew that the reason was he'd come to care for Bliss. More than he'd wanted to. And a helluva lot more than he'd planned.

He'd thought he was so clever, weaving his web of intrigue to capture Bliss Fortune. The problem was, he'd never expected to get caught in a snare of his own making.

"I suppose the next item of business is to pay Churchill a visit."

"That would be my suggestion. However, since he's left New Orleans for his store in Savannah, I'd suggest you wait until tomorrow. One more day isn't going to make a difference at this point."

"It sure as hell will if he leaves the country."

"True. But I'll put one of my other men on him for now." Cunningham leaned back in his chair and plucked at an imaginary speck of lint on his impeccably creased chalk gray suit trousers. "I assume you'd like a day to try to make personal amends with Ms. Fortune."

Shayne's eyes narrowed suspiciously. In the three years they'd worked together, he'd never witnessed a single human emotion from his superior. "What's the catch?"

"There's no catch, O'Malley. Believe it or not, I've been in your situation before." Cunningham's eyes turned reminiscent as he lit a cigar. "It was during the height of the Cold War and she was a Russian agent I'd been assigned to recruit. I'm afraid I allowed my emotions to overrule my head in that case."

"What happened?"

"Not only did she turn down my professional offer to become a double agent, she rejected my proposal, as well. Then threatened to turn my name over to her superiors, which effectively took me out of the Soviet spy-catching business."

"Is she still in the business?"

A brief shadow moved across Cunningham's gun-metal gray eyes. "I believe I heard she died in a plane crash a few months later."

Shayne knew that if he asked the all-important question—whether or not the crash had been an accident—Cunningham would undoubtedly lie. Not that he could blame him. They were all liars; it was what they were paid to do.

When he'd first started working in the shadowy world of the Company, with the ink still wet on the diploma granting him dual degrees in international relations and business, Shayne had been proud of his ability to make anyone believe anything. He was, his superiors had told him, a creative and gifted dissembler.

Inevitably, after a time the initial kick wore off, but he

never lost the inner drive to get better and better at his job. And on those rare, fleeting occasions when he'd wonder if the ends justified his admittedly shady means, Shayne had closed his mind to any introspection.

He no longer believed, as he had in those heady early days, that he was saving the free world. But neither had he been overly disturbed by his actions. It was a job, no different from any other. A job he just happened to be very, very good at.

And then he'd met Bliss, who, even without knowing she was doing it, had chipped away at the rock he'd encased his conscience in, exposing it to the blinding light of day, forcing him to take a long hard look at not only what he was doing, but who he'd become.

Unfortunately, Shayne didn't like what he saw. And now, comparing Cunningham with his oldest brother, he realized that Mike had been right to challenge him when he'd first hit town. Michael O'Malley had always been one of the good guys; now Shayne realized that somehow, when he wasn't paying close attention, he'd become one of the bad guys. Or at least, one of the not-so-good guys.

He was going to change that, he decided as he left the hotel room. But first he had to straighten things out with Bliss.

ZELDA ANSWERED THE DOOR. "You're Shayne O'Malley." She gave him a long hard look that reminded him uncomfortably of Sister Immaculata, the harridan who'd made an entire class of nine-year-old boys miserable back in the third grade.

"Yes, ma'am, I am," he answered in his most polite voice. If he'd had a hat, he would have tipped it.

"You realize, of course, that you've broken my granddaughter's heart."

He'd known that. He'd seen it on Bliss's face, heard it in her trembling voice. But to hear the accusation stated out loud tore at some elemental fiber deep inside him.

"Yes, ma'am. And I'm really sorry about that."

Zelda gave him another long look that gave Shayne the impression she could see all the way to his soul. "I was about to fix myself some iced tea. Would you like some?"

"Yes, ma'am." Shayne didn't bother to hide his relief that he had, at least, made his way past the dragon guarding the door. Of course the treasure—namely Bliss—was still a very long way out of reach. "That would hit the spot. Thank you."

She lead the way to a sun-filled room, decorated with chintz-covered wicker furniture, which overlooked a garden that was a riotous display of bright spring color. "I'll be right back."

"Thank you," Shayne repeated humbly, continuing to feel like a tongue-tied nine-year-old.

Although he tried to tell himself that it was merely his imagination working overtime, or merely wishful thinking, as he sat alone in the cheerful room, watching the butterflies flit from flower to flower, Shayne thought he sensed Bliss's presence.

"Bliss decorated this room, didn't she?" he asked Zelda, when she returned with a white wicker glass-bottomed tray and two tall glasses.

"She found the furniture at a flea market in Houma." Zelda handed him a glass. "Sewed the covers for the cushions herself." The wicker creaked as she sat down in the lounge chair. "The garden's mine."

"You and my mother would get along great. Gardening has always been her avocation. I remember her saying that when you're working in your garden, you're closer to heaven than anywhere else on earth."

Zelda nodded her copper-bright head. "Sounds as if your mother is a wise woman. Makes me wonder how she managed to rear such an idiot for a son."

"I've been wondering the same thing lately." Shayne took a drink of the tea, which proved to be freshly brewed and sprigged with mint. "This is great."

"I've always believed if you're going to do something, you ought to take the time to do it right. So, did you really think my granddaughter was a jewel thief?"

"No, ma'am." Although his initial reaction had been to lie, Shayne reminded himself that he'd vowed to turn over a new leaf. "At least not in the end."

"I do hope you'd at least decided she was innocent before you took her to bed."

"Yes, ma'am." Shayne was uncomfortable discussing sex with a woman old enough to be his own grandmother, but understood that they were on Zelda's turf, which meant that if he had any chance of recruiting her help in winning Bliss back, he was going to have to play the game her way.

"Do you love my granddaughter?"

This was worse than talking about sex. "I care for Bliss a great deal."

"That wasn't what I asked." Zelda's bright blue eyes bored into his like lasers. "You know, of course, that Bliss is in love with you."

"Yes, ma'am."

"So, before I decide whether or not I should press your case, I need to know if you feel the same way about her. Though I hate to speak ill of the dead, Alan Fortune was a conniving rat. But he only wounded Bliss's pride. You broke her heart."

"I realize that, ma'am." It was difficult, having his behavior thrown back in his face this way, but Shayne knew he deserved it. He'd also crawl buck naked down Bourbon Street during the height of Mardi Gras if that's what it took to win Bliss back. "And, although it doesn't change things, I'm ashamed that I didn't handle things differently from the beginning."

"That's the trouble with lies," Zelda said sagely. "Once you get one started, it just rolls away from you, getting bigger and bigger as it goes...

"So," she repeated, "do you love Bliss?"

Shayne decided that if there was ever a time for honesty, this was it. "I don't know," he admitted reluctantly. "I can tell you that I've never felt about any other woman the way I do about your granddaughter."

"My Dupree always said he knew the minute he saw me that he loved me."

"Obviously your husband was smarter than me."

"Not smarter, just more in touch with his feelings, perhaps," Zelda mused. "Known a lot of women, have you?"

Shayne flinched a bit at that question and wondered if Bliss was hiding out anywhere nearby, listening to this cross-examination. "Yes ma'am, I'm afraid I have."

"You don't have to apologize. I'd be worried if a good-looking single man like you hadn't sown his share of wild oats. But the time comes when a boy needs to grow up. Become a man. And settle down."

"I'm ready to do that." As soon as he heard the words leave his mouth, Shayne knew that was the truth. "I didn't realize until just recently how much New Orleans meant to me. And how homesick I'd become."

"Sometimes it takes a while to discover that happiness is best found in your own backyard," Zelda agreed. "Bliss thought she'd love jet-setting around the country. But even if Alan hadn't been such a louse, she would have gotten tired of that high life real soon."

"I've never met a woman who was more comfortable—and happy—with her life." At least she'd been happy, until she'd gone to a party in Paris and met him.

"She'll be that way again," Zelda said, as if she could read his mind. "Bliss has a knack for bouncing back from adversity. My Dupree was like that. Lord knows, that man failed at everything he tried, but he never stopped getting excited about the idea of winning the jackpot."

"I think he did that, Ms. Zelda. When he fell in love with you." Shayne had never said a more truthful statement in his life.

Zelda laughed at that, a rich musical laugh that reminded him a great deal of Bliss. Then again, Shayne told himself, these days everything reminded him of Bliss.

"That's exactly what you're supposed to say." Her cheeks dimpled and her eyes twinkled merrily. "You are quite a charmer, Shayne O'Malley. In that respect you're a great deal different from your brother."

Shayne suspected Zelda hadn't just given him a compliment. "Mike's always been plainspoken."

"Solid as a rock, that man," Zelda agreed. "I suppose, since we're laying all our cards on the table, I should admit that I'd hoped Bliss would fall in love with Michael."

"That probably would have been better for her," Shayne reluctantly admitted.

"There was a time, after Alan, when I would have

thought so. Now, I believe I may have been wrong about that." Zelda put her glass down on the lacy iron table beside her chair. "Bliss is still feeling the sting of your falsehoods. You must understand that, after Alan, it must seem like a case of history repeating itself for her."

"I understand. But appearances to the contrary, I'm nothing like Alan Fortune. Not really."

"I can see that. And I know Bliss will, too, once she has time to think about it. Which is what you need to do, Shayne. Give her time." She stood up, effectively signaling an end to the conversation. "In the meantime, I'll do whatever I can to convince her to at least talk with you."

"Thank you, ma'am."

"I'm doing it for Bliss, not you. She may appear to be a carefree, blithe spirit, but she also has a steely core, which has allowed her to survive life's little challenges. She can also be remarkably hardheaded. It's not going to be easy, winning her over. But she's a clever girl and if we all gang up on her, eventually, I know she'll see the light."

Shayne could have kissed the older woman. In fact, acting on impulse, as he so seldom did, he ignored her outstretched hand, took hold of her softly padded shoulders and touched his smiling lips to her remarkably unwrinkled cheek.

"I can see why Bliss's grandfather fell head over heels in love with you," he said.

She blushed prettily, which took a good ten years off her age and reminded Shayne yet again of Bliss.

"A charmer," she repeated. "But then, so was Dupree. And that man gave me the most wonderful years of my life." Her twinkling eyes turned resolute. "I expect you to do the same for my Bliss."

"Yes, ma'am," Shayne agreed without hesitation.

The conversation hadn't turned out as well as he'd hoped—he'd fantasized about Bliss running into the room, tearfully flinging herself into his arms and forgiving him—but at least, as he left the cozy little carriage house, Shayne felt more optimistic than he had in a very long time.

So deep in thought was Shayne as he approached the Jag parked at the curb, he didn't see Bliss standing at an upstairs window, her cheeks stained with tears as she watched him walk away.

BOTH HIS BROTHERS were waiting in the gilt-and-marble lobby of the Whitfield Palace when Shayne returned to the hotel.

"Hey, kid." Roarke punched him in the upper arm, the blow hard enough it took all Shayne's self-control not to flinch. "So, how long were you going to be in town before you decided to look up your favorite brother?"

"Things were complicated." His arm was stinging but there was no way Shayne was going to give Roarke the satisfaction of rubbing it. Sometimes, he thought, it stunk being the youngest brother.

"Yeah, Mike's filled me in. Too bad about you and Bliss."

"That'll work out," Shayne assured both brothers, who exchanged a look at the news.

"Does that mean you've talked with her?" Michael asked.

"Not yet. But Zelda and I had a long discussion about my intentions. And she's on my side."

"That's gotta help," Roarke said. "Bliss thinks the world of her grandmother."

"And rightfully so," Mike said.

"I can't argue with that. She seems like a dynamite lady," Shayne agreed.

"Bliss will probably be a lot like Zelda when she's a little old lady," Roarke suggested. "A guy could do a lot worse than spend his golden years with a woman like that."

There was no way he was going to respond to the innuendo in his brother's voice. "Speaking of golden years, I hear you're thinking of settling down."

"You've heard right. I've given up my roaming ways, hung up my rambling shoes and set up housekeeping with the woman of my dreams. Which reminds me, I'm supposed to ask you both what you're doing the first Saturday in September."

"I don't have anything scheduled yet," Mike answered. "Is Daria planning a Labor Day party?"

"In a way." Roarke's grin was the same one he'd used to charm his way past heavily armed border guards during innumerable faraway wars. "We're getting married."

"Married?" Shayne stared at his brother. This was even worse than he'd feared. Then again, he decided, looking at the smug, entirely satisfied expression on Roarke's face, perhaps it wasn't so bad, after all.

"Damn, I knew it!" It was Mike's turn to punch Roarke. "Congratulations, little brother. You're getting a real gem."

"I know that." Roarke's grin flashed white in his darkly tanned face.

"And let me be the first to warn you," Mike continued, "that if you don't treat Daria like she deserves, I'm going to punch your lights out."

"I'd expect no less," Roarke agreed easily.

"So," Shayne said, "when do I get to meet this paragon?"

"Tomorrow."

"Why not tonight?"

"Because," Roarke said patiently, "tonight we're going to go out on the town and drink to my upcoming nuptials. And, given the miserable romantic mess you've managed to get yourself into, you're allowed to get rip-roaring drunk to drown your sorrows."

"You're all heart."

"Hey," Roarke grinned and punched him again, "that's what big brothers are for."

They eschewed the lavishly decorated Blue Bayou Lounge, settling instead for a homey Irish pub on Bourbon Street. Shayne had just started on his second Guinness when Mike's cellular phone rang.

"I have to run back to the hotel," he announced after the brief conversation. "A package just arrived for me there."

"At the hotel? Why not your office?"

"Because after Fortune's death, I'm not certain that building's as secure as it should be. And since I didn't know where, exactly, we'd end up tonight, it seemed easier to have it delivered there."

"What is it?" Roarke asked.

"Does it have something to do with Fortune?" Shayne inquired at the same time.

"It should be a package of photographs from a friend of mine at a clipping service based in Atlanta. Apparently Fortune used the same service to keep track of how often—and where—his name showed up in print. She promised to pull the information and courier it to me."

"Good thinking." Shayne took a long swallow and

wiped the foam off his upper lip with the back of his hand. "I'm impressed."

"I don't know why you should be," Mike stated. "I am, after all, a private detective."

"I knew that." Shayne grinned. "I just wasn't sure you were any good."

He ducked the fist headed toward his jaw just in time. Still grinning, he tossed off the last of the smooth dark brew and left the pub with his brothers.

"Sorry to screw up your celebration," he told Roarke as they walked back to the hotel.

"That's okay. We'll have other nights. I'm not going anywhere. And neither, it appears, are you."

Shayne heard the question in his brother's tone. "I figured I might hang around town for a while," he said with careful casualness.

"Bliss hooked him," Mike said to Roarke.

"Looks as if our baby brother has it bad," Roarke said to Mike.

Shayne's only response was a muttered curse.

THE PHOTOS ONLY documented what Shayne had already known. That Alan Fortune knew a lot of women. There were shots of him in Monaco with a divorced heir to an Oklahoma oil fortune, several of him skiing in Switzerland with the former wife of a Wall Street tycoon, and one of him dancing at a Manhattan club with a black-leather-clad performance actress who lived off a trust fund from her Philadelphia DAR grandmother.

"This one is interesting," Roarke said, drawing their attention to a clipping from the *New Orleans Times-Picayune.*

"It's Bliss's wedding photo," Mike said.

Shayne took hold of the clipping and stared down at the young woman who was gazing up at her husband. She looked so young. No, not young, he decided, innocent.

Shayne had never realized that he was a jealous man until he'd met Bliss. But even though he'd come to terms with the unfamiliar, uncomfortable emotion, he felt a sense of relief that he didn't see the same light of love in her gaze as she looked up at her groom that had been there when he'd made love to her.

"She sure is drop-dead gorgeous," Roarke murmured. "If I wasn't an engaged man, Shayne, I just might have to give you a run for your money."

"And I just might have to knock your block off for messin' with my woman."

"Your woman?" Roarke challenged. "I hadn't realized you'd made a committment to the lady, yet."

"That still doesn't give you the right—"

"Hey, you two," Mike complained. "If you could both just grow up for a minute, can I remind you that we have a job to do?" He put another photo clipping down on the coffee table. "Here's one of Fortune and that other antique dealer."

"Churchill," Shayne answered.

"That's him," Mike agreed.

The shot appeared to have been taken aboard a ship docked in what Shayne recognized as the harbor at Cannes. The two men were sitting at a table on the deck, playing cards.

"Wait a minute," he said, looking at the woman who was standing behind Alan, her hand, adorned with a huge diamond, resting on his shoulder. "I know her."

"Really?" Mike leaned closer. "Who is she?"

"I don't know her name. But I saw her talking to Fortune in Paris." Scenes shifted, then slipped into place. "At the party."

"Where the jewels were stolen? The same party where you met Bliss?"

"That's it. She was also talking to Churchill in the parking lot after yesterday's auction." Obviously they were looking at the woman who'd lifted the necklace from the Paris apartment. Presumably for Nigel Churchill.

"I told you it wasn't Bliss," Mike said.

Ignoring him, Shayne leaned closer. "Who's that in the background? He looks familiar."

Mike squinted. "It's too blurry to tell."

"Try this." Roarke pulled a red Swiss army knife out of his pocket and unfolded a miniature magnifying glass. "It's not much, but it might help."

Shayne held it up to the paper, cursing as the photo remained indistinct. But as he drew it slightly away, he experienced a jolt of recognition.

"My God," he said. "It's Cunningham."

"Who's Cunningham?" Roarke asked.

Mike and Shayne exchanged a grim look. "My boss," Shayne answered as he reached for the phone and began punching the lucite buttons with more force than necessary.

"I know you told me to give her some time," he said, after Bliss's grandmother answered, "but this is an emergency. It's about Fortune's murder.... What?"

His hand made a frustrated swipe through his hair. "What the hell was she thinking of, to go back there—"

"Let me." Mike grabbed the phone from his brother. "Zelda, how are you sweetheart? That's great. Now, I don't want to get you worried, because everything's going to be all right, but I'm going to hang up now so

Roarke, Shayne and I can head over to The Treasure Trove. And what I'd like you to do is call 911, and tell the dispatch operator that I told you to have them send a squad car over to the shop. And tell them I said we might have a possible hostage situation.

"No," he said quickly, calmly, "don't get upset, darlin'. You know I'd never let anything happen to Bliss. She's going to be just fine. It's just that we might need a little additional help from the cavalry, okay?"

He nodded at the answer from the other end of the line. "That's my girl. Now, you stay put, and we'll be bringing your granddaughter home safe and sound real soon."

He hung up the phone and turned to his brothers who were already waiting at the door. "Let's go."

13

BLISS WASN'T AT ALL EAGER to face the mess left behind by Alan's death. But on the other hand, she'd been going crazy, sitting alone in her room thinking about Shayne, reliving everything he'd said to her since their first meeting in Paris, remembering every look, every touch, the way her bones melted and her blood flamed whenever he touched her.

Finally, she couldn't take it anymore and had explained to Zelda that she needed to get the shop cleaned up so she could open in the morning. She also hoped that physical work would take her mind off the man she'd mistakenly fallen in love with.

It hadn't been easy, slipping away without the bodyguard Michael had assigned to her sitting in a car across the street from the carriage house. Fortunately, during her teenage years, she'd discovered a gap in the hedge, which she'd used on the rare occasions she'd sneaked out of the house to go down to the Quarter with friends. The opening in the hedge led into the backyard of the house next door. From there it had been a simple matter to escape detection.

"How could he do it?" she murmured as she unlocked the door to The Treasure Trove and turned off the alarm that certainly hadn't kept Alan out of her office. Michael had been right when he'd tried to get her to upgrade the system. Once she was willing to talk to him again, she'd have to ask him to do whatever it took to secure the store.

"How could he make love to me when everything between us was nothing but a lie?"

"Not everything," a deep voice murmured just as she turned on the overhead lights.

"What are you doing here?" She glared at Cunningham. If he thought she was going to subject herself to more interrogation, he had another think coming.

Bliss was about to insist that he leave her shop before she called the police when she noticed the ugly blued steel gun he was holding in his hand. The pistol that was, unbelievably, pointed her way.

"Waiting for you, of course."

She could survive this, Bliss assured herself. The thing to do was to remain calm. "How did you know I'd come back tonight?"

"O'Malley has spent weeks filling me in on your every move. And before that, Alan used to talk about you frequently."

"You knew Alan?"

"Quite well, actually."

"You were friends?" That came as a shock. As dislikable as she'd found Cunningham earlier, Bliss had, at least, thought the government agent was supposed to be one of the good guys.

"More like business acquaintances. But our shared interests put us in situations where men tend to discuss—and compare—women. Alan had a great many flaws, but you proved to be his fatal one."

"I don't understand." This was one more horrible revelation in a day filled with unpleasant surprises.

"When he found out that Churchill and I were going to frame you for the earlier robberies that had been driv-

ing our government and Interpol crazy over the past
year, he displayed an unfortunate tendency to play the
white knight, by trying to get you to get rid of the necklace so it wouldn't be found in your shop."

"He never said that."

"He couldn't, without implicating himself. But unfortunately, what he didn't realize was that he ended up
putting you in even more danger."

"I don't understand." The headache that had sub-
sided to the back of her head came pounding forward
again, almost blinding in its intensity.

"You know too much."

"I don't know a damn thing!" Frustrated, and frightened, she dragged her hand through her hair.

"That's what you said earlier. But you see, we
couldn't take the chance."

"We?" *Oh, please,* she begged whatever fates had decided to play this horrendous joke on her, *don't let
Shayne be mixed up in this, too.*

"Churchill and I." He smiled. "You were afraid I was
referring to O'Malley."

"I don't want to talk about him." On this, at least, Bliss
was on firm ground.

"Fine. Let's talk about what Alan told you. And what
you might have passed on to O'Malley."

Bliss suddenly realized that in a misguided attempt to
save her from being arrested, Alan had put not only his
life, and hers, in jeopardy, but that Shayne was in danger, as well. Looking at the implacable cruelty in the
government agent's eyes, she had not a single doubt that
if this man believed he was a suspect in the robberies
and murder, he'd kill Shayne O'Malley without a second thought.

"I didn't tell Agent O'Malley anything. We didn't discuss Alan."

"I find that difficult to believe. After all, you were intimate with O'Malley. And he was investigating both you and your former husband. Surely he questioned you about him?"

"He tried. But my marriage was not exactly a happy time in my life. I didn't want to talk about it."

Cunningham lifted a patently disbelieving brow. "And you expect me to believe that was the end of it?"

"It's the truth."

"O'Malley's not accustomed to letting anyone else call the shots." He rubbed his jaw thoughtfully and gave her a longer, more intense perusal. "I do believe, Ms. Fortune, that he might have let himself get emotionally involved with you."

Bliss didn't want to allow herself to consider that possibility. Because if she did, she'd have to consider forgiving Shayne. And that was one thing she was definitely not prepared to do.

When she didn't answer, Cunningham brought the subject back to his original reason for having broken into her shop in the first place.

"If Fortune didn't fill you in on all the details, then why did you get rid of the bear?" he asked.

"What bear?" She automatically glanced over toward the locked cabinet of stuffed animals.

"The Steiff bear you bought in Paris."

"Oh, that one. I didn't get rid of it. I sold it. The very day it arrived. To a German tourist." Comprehension sank in. "The jewels were inside it?"

"Clever girl." He shook his head with mock regret. "That was, indeed, unfortunate timing for us."

"Shayne was supposed to find them," Bliss guessed.

"And arrest me, which would take the heat off the real thieves."

"That was the original plan. But you know what they say about the best-laid plans of mice and men." His smile was as cold and deadly as an alligator's. "At least the jewels in question were merely paste."

So that's what Alan had been talking about. A new, even more horrendous thought suddenly occurred to Bliss. Alan had discussed the jewels with Zelda. What if Cunningham knew that? What if he also intended to kill her grandmother?

Over my dead body, Bliss vowed, hoping desperately it wouldn't come to that.

"Why?" she asked, wanting to keep the man talking until she could figure some way out of this mess. "Why would you get involved with Nigel in the first place?"

"For the money, of course," he said. "When I first discovered Churchill's little theft ring, I decided I had two choices. I could turn him in to the authorities, who'd put him behind bars. Or, I could let him know that he'd just taken on a partner."

"That's despicable."

"It's not as if we were stealing from widows and orphans. Or the church poor box," he reminded her. "The people who owned the jewelry could well afford to replace it. And besides, they were insured."

"Now I understand why my rates are so high," she muttered.

Before he could respond to that, a siren sounded outside. A moment later, a voice came over an electronic bullhorn, letting Cunningham know that the police had surrounded the shop.

"Damn," he snarled, "this has got to be O'Malley's doing." He grabbed her by the arm, pressed the barrel of the pistol against her temple, and began pushing her toward her back office.

"What are you going to do?"

"That should be obvious." He'd recaptured his composure and now seemed almost matter-of-fact. "We're going to play 'Let's Make a Deal.' And you, my dear, are the prize behind door number three."

"DAMN!" SHAYNE POUNDED his fist into his palm. "I should have realized it was Cunningham."

"Don't be so hard on yourself," Roarke said. "Why would you have any reason to suspect him?"

"How about the little fact that I always knew the guy was pond scum?"

"That goes without saying. He's a spook, isn't he?"

Shayne knew his brother's insult was meant to garner a reaction, to make him stop hating himself. But that wasn't about to happen anytime soon, and if any harm came to Bliss, Shayne knew he'd never forgive himself.

"It's going to be all right," Michael said. "The guy knows there's no way out. He's going to have to let Bliss go."

Shayne wished he could be so optimistic. "You don't know Cunningham. He's like your average rat—push him into a corner, and he's going to bare his teeth and fight."

There had to be some way out to get Bliss out of this, he thought. But how?

BLISS HAD NEVER been more terrified in her life. But she did not intend to give up without a fight. She was sure that Cunningham had no intention of spending the rest of his life in prison. He'd take his own life, first. But, although she'd be disinclined to shed any tears over this man's death, the trick was to keep him from taking her with him.

He was pushing her across the floor, the sweaty hand on her back revealing he was not as cool, calm and collected as outward appearances would lead one to believe. As they approached the counter, she suddenly had an idea.

Without stopping to consider the risk, she wrenched free and dropped to her knees, landing right in the middle of the bloodstain she'd come here to clean up.

"What the hell?" Before he could react, she'd rolled behind the counter, pulled out the canister of pepper spray and sent a toxic cloud into the murderous agent's face.

As he coughed, violently, she jumped up, grabbed a heavy sterling silver loving cup and brought it down on top of his head. Unfortunately, in order to hit him, then race past him to the door, she had to run through the pepper spray cloud herself.

As she burst out of the store, she was coughing as violently as Cunningham.

SHAYNE WATCHED as the door to The Treasure Trove suddenly burst open. Then, as if the action were taking place in slow motion, he saw the gathered police officers all lift their pistols in unison.

"Hold your fire!" he shouted, just a second before the police sergeant. "It's not your killer."

Risking getting shot himself, he raced toward Bliss, took her into his arms and dragged her behind one of the squad cars.

"Let...go..." Dammit, her lungs felt as if they were on fire. "Let go of me!"

Shayne wasn't about to do that. Not in this lifetime. "Are you all right?"

"What...do—" more coughing "—you think?" she gasped. Her eyes were tearing painfully from the cayenne pepper. "Do I look like I'm okay?"

Michael was squatting down beside her. "What happened, sweetheart?"

"Pepper...spray." Bliss dragged in a harsh breath, then wished she hadn't as it burned all the way down. "I zapped him with...the stuff you and Zelda insisted I get."

"Good girl."

Much, much later, Bliss would look back on Michael's behavior and decide that it said something about his nature that he could laugh at such a terrifying time. But at the moment, all she could concentrate on was trying to breathe. And fighting against the very strong impulse just to stay forever in Shayne O'Malley's strong, comforting arms.

"Don't talk anymore," Michael suggested. "Not until we get you to a hospital and get you checked out."

"I don't want to go to any hospital."

"Lord, you are one stubborn female," he muttered. "But this time, you're outmatched, Bliss. Because if need be, all three O'Malley brothers will sit on you until you agree."

She continued to cough as she looked up at them, a solid, unyielding wall of resistance. Knowing when she'd met her match, she shrugged.

"I won't stay."

"That's up to the doctor," Shayne said.

Although it was difficult, considering he still had his arms around her shoulders, Bliss managed to ignore him.

"I'm not staying," she said again.

An hour later, she was sitting on a cold metal table behind a curtain in Tulane Hospital and Medical Center's emergency room. Roarke had been dispatched to go to the carriage house and assure Zelda that Bliss was going to be all right, Michael was still right beside her, where he'd been since he'd carried her through the hospital's automatic doors, and Shayne, apparently, was wearing the tile thin pacing the waiting room floor.

"I owe you my life," she told Michael. She'd managed to stop coughing, and although it still burned her lungs to breathe, she was feeling a great deal better.

"You're the one who nuked Cunningham," he reminded her.

"But I'm betting you're the one who called the police in the first place, which kept him from just shooting me on the spot."

"I told Zelda to call the cops," Michael admitted. "But if Shayne hadn't dragged me into his cockamamy investigation, we never would have discovered Cunningham's involvement."

Michael had received a call from a friend on the police force, who'd told him that the government agent, when faced with arrest, had, as Bliss had feared he might, taken his own life.

"If Shayne hadn't dragged me into his cockamamy investigation, all this wouldn't have happened," Bliss said. "And Cunningham and Alan would still be alive."

"Perhaps Cunningham," Michael agreed. "But Alan was too much of a loose cannon to have survived for long. And it wasn't Shayne who put you at the center of everything, Bliss. The thefts had become too high-profile these past months. It was Churchill and Cunningham who were looking for someone to take the fall to effectively put the case to rest."

"So they chose me."

"Since your semiannual trip to Paris came just when they were looking for someone to frame, and since you'd been a thorn in Churchill's side by refusing to sell him your shop, you were the logical choice. That way he killed two birds with one stone. Metaphorically speaking."

"Not so metaphorically," she murmured, thinking that two men were now dead. And for what? Some pretty rocks. It seemed so pointless.

Her shoulders sagged. She was suddenly so very tired. "Can I go home now?"

"Absolutely. I'll go get the doc and see if we can speed up the paperwork." He paused. "Shayne's been going nuts out there. I don't suppose..."

"No." She shook her head with renewed force. "I don't want to see him."

Although he looked inclined to argue, Bliss was grateful when Michael merely shrugged. "Your call," he said mildly. Then left her alone to ponder yet again why she couldn't have fallen in love with the steady, trustworthy O'Malley brother.

THE NEXT THIRTY DAYS were the longest Shayne had ever lived through. Bliss, proving as stubborn as Zelda had predicted, had refused to take his calls or answer his letters. She'd also returned every single present he'd sent to her—chocolates, flowers, a plush pink-and-purple alligator, an antique perfume bottle alleged to have belonged to Marie Antoinette. But even the knowing smirk of the delivery service kid who returned the gifts to him every day hadn't stopped Shayne from trying.

He'd had to make three trips back to Washington to testify regarding his superior. The more he spoke about the work they'd done together, the more he realized that in believing anyone was fair game, and the end justified the means to close a case, he'd put his integrity in cold storage.

He tried to explain his feelings the day he resigned.

"Are you certain you want to do this, O'Malley?" the Washington bureau chief asked.

"Positive, sir." Shayne laid his badge on the polished mahogany desk that had once belonged to Patrick Henry.

"We need a man to take Cunningham's place. I recommended you."

A recommendation from this man would cinch the deal. There'd been a time when Shayne would have jumped at the chance to actually set policy. Cunningham had been near the peak of a very exclusive pyramid; he'd been mostly free of oversight from Washington, which was how he'd managed to become a rogue agent in the first place. And although Shayne knew he'd never turn into a thief or murderer, what he'd done to Bliss—the behavior he'd somehow managed to justify to himself—was proof that he'd been on a very slippery slope for a long time. It was true: Power definitely tended to corrupt.

"I'm flattered, sir. But I'm afraid I couldn't be of any use to the agency any longer."

"Why not? The excellent job you did exposing Cunningham and shutting down that theft ring that was driving us all crazy proves you're on the top of your game."

Shayne decided there was no point in trying to explain that he was going on a hunt for his conscience.

"You know what they say, sir, that you should always go out on top."

He grinned, his patent, professional smile, shook hands with the silver-haired man on the other side of the desk and left the office.

THE FOLLOWING MORNING Shayne was in what his brother laughingly called an office, going through what only a generous person could call the accounting books.

"How the hell do you know if you're making money or losing it?" he asked, trying to make some sense of the rows of green columns.

"Simple. If my checks don't bounce and I have a balance in the checkbook at the end of the month, I'm making money. If I have to go into my credit reserve, which doesn't happen all that often, I'm behind."

"You charge different rates for different clients?"

"Different circumstances."

"What about this one? You marked it paid in full."

"So?"

"So, I can't see a record of any check coming in."

"That's probably because there wasn't any."

"The guy paid cash?"

"No."

"Money order?"

"No. I did the work gratis."

"For free?" Shayne looked up at Mike in disbelief. "Why?"

"The guy's a cop. He once saved my ass during a riot in the St. Louis Number One cemetery. I owed him, big time, so when his youngest son started hanging out with gangs, I dragged the kid out to the state prison, let some of the cons I'd arrested over the years scream in his face, then, after the scared-straight lecture, took him home. He's back in school, bucking for honor roll."

"My brother, Saint Michael, the P.I."

"I told you, I owed the guy a favor. I realize you've been operating in another world, but in my little corner of the globe, friends look out for friends."

"Same thing in my world," Shayne muttered. "You watch out so some friend doesn't stick a knife between your ribs."

"Sounds like you could use a better class of friends."

"That's the same thing I was thinking." Shayne looked up from the ledger sheets. "Looks as if you could use a business planner."

"They cost money."

"True. But if you asked real nice, I'd probably be willing to give you a family rate."

Michael didn't look all that surprised. He crossed his legs at the ankles, folded his arms over his chest and leaned back against the gray steel filing cabinet that was in desperate need of reorganization. "Are you asking for a job?"

"I guess I am."

Mike rubbed his chin and appeared to be giving that some thought. "I don't think it'd work out."

"Why the hell not? If you think I can't do the job—"

"Hey, I saw your college transcripts, remember? You got nearly straight As. I have no doubt you're a whiz at your work, but I can't see you taking orders from me."

Truthfully, that had been the one little problem that had been nagging at Shayne all the way home from Washington. "We won't know if we don't try."

Having given it a great deal of thought, he also couldn't see Mike being too outrageously bossy. Now Roarke, on the other hand, was another matter. Although he loved his brother and knew Roarke felt the same, Shayne figured they could probably work five minutes together before they started breaking furniture.

"How about I make another suggestion," Mike said.

"What?"

"I think it might work out better if we were partners."

The idea was immediately appealing. "I'll want to pay my fair share to buy in."

"That isn't necessary."

"It is for me."

"Fine." Michael's lips twitched as if he were trying to hold back a grin. "I know you said you wanted out of the spy business, but how would you feel about working on some investigations from time to time?"

"I'd enjoy that." Knowing that Michael would never stoop to the tactics Shayne had vowed never to use again, he accepted the offer.

"Okay. I guess that settles it." Michael held out his hand. As Shayne shook it, he thought how terrific it felt, going to work with his brother.

"Let's call up Roarke," Michael suggested. "We can pick up our celebration night where we left off."

"In a minute." Shayne pulled a piece of paper from his pocket. "I need your signature, confirming that I'm gainfully employed."

Michael perused the paper. "You're buying a house?"

"Yep." Shayne's look challenged his brother to say a single negative word.

"Cool," was the word Michael chose as he signed the paper.

Cool, Shayne thought as they left the office to meet Roarke at the pub. He now had a job and a house. Two down, one to go.

"DAMN, DAMN, DAMN." Bliss twisted the key in the ignition, frustrated when the engine absolutely refused to turn over.

Michael, returning to his office after a stakeout, found Bliss glaring down into the open hood of her car.

"Need some help?"

"I don't suppose you know anything about car engines."

"Just enough to call the auto club," Michael lied. He was uncomfortable with the prevarication, but was willing, just this one time, to do it. And it was, after all, he reminded himself, for Bliss's own good.

"I'll have to call a cab. I promised I'd be home in time for dinner."

She did not add what Michael already knew; that she'd been working overtime in an attempt to keep her mind off Shayne. Which was difficult since he was now working for Michael. She'd actually considered evicting the detective agency, but decided there was no way she was going to allow Shayne to realize she was still hurting. So, he used the back door, which kept him out of her shop, and whenever their paths happened to cross, neither spoke. Not even to mention the steady stream of gifts that she continued to return. Except for yesterday's. Which had, unfortunately, proven too irresistible.

She'd have to give it back, of course, she'd decided. She didn't want to give him the wrong idea, that there was a place for him in her life.

"Why don't you let me give you a lift?" Michael suggested easily. "Since I'm going in that direction, anyway."

"Are you sure? I wouldn't want to take you out of your way."

"Hey," he smiled and skimmed his finger down the slope of her nose, "that's what friends are for.

"That's better," he said when she returned his smile with a faint one of her own.

"What's better?"

"You finally smiled at me. I thought it might be another month before you'd forgive me enough to get to that point."

"I forgave you a long time ago."

"But not Shayne."

"It's hard," she murmured, looking away from the handsome face that so reminded her of the man she loved.

"For him, too," Michael dared.

She sighed. "I know." She'd seen the frustration and the need in his eyes, whenever their gazes accidentally met. "Lilah certainly seems to have taken him under her wing."

"Lilah's a friendly woman."

"Yes." Bliss's tone was dry as she wondered, yet again, exactly how friendly Lilah Middleton had been to their new tenant. She cast a significant glance down at her watch. "Well, if I'm going to be home on time—"

"We'd better get going," Michael finished up for her. He closed the hood, feeling not the slightest bit guilty about the starter solenoid deep in his pocket.

Their relationship was almost back to normal. Conversation flowed easily as they drove from the French Quarter, Michael telling her about today's stakeout, Bliss telling him about an upcoming auction she was excited about attending.

"There's a pair of Regency chairs that I'm dying to have. Churchill outbid me for them in Lafayette, but now that the government's selling off all his stuff, I've got a second chance at them."

"I have not a doubt in the world you'll get them."

"I love a man with confidence."

"I have confidence in you, Bliss. In your remarkable capacity for bouncing back from adversity, your generous and forgiving heart—"

"I said I didn't want to talk about Shayne."

"We're not. We're talking about you," he reminded her mildly as he pulled up in front of a Queen Anne Victorian that brought to mind a gingerbread house. It was badly in need of a coat of paint and the steps to the front porch looked downright dangerous, but Bliss could definitely see the house's potential.

"What's this?"

"A house I wanted you to look at for me."

"Oh?" Her interest, already piqued, rose. "Are you thinking of buying it?"

"That's up in the air right now. But I could use some expert advice."

She glanced down at her watch again. She really didn't want to disappoint Zelda, but the lure of this darling house was irresistible.

"I have time for a quick walk-through. But I'm no expert on construction. You'll need a contractor for that."

"It's already passed inspection," he revealed as he took her arm and guided her up the rickety steps that would definitely need to be replaced. "The foundation's firm and there's not a termite on the premises. The structure's solid as a rock, and all the windows can stay if they're reglazed. The only major thing is the roof, which needs to be replaced."

"Lucky you."

He didn't answer. Instead, he merely unlocked the carved door with the lovely etched glass fanlight, and invited her into the house.

Although it was getting toward evening, the sun was still high enough in the sky to bathe the front foyer with a warm, golden glow. "The floor's magnificent," she murmured, struck with an urge to bend down and run her fingers over the gleaming mahogany planks. The house appeared empty, her words echoed in the stillness.

"It's original. If you think this is great, wait until you see the upstairs bedroom." He gestured toward the narrow stairway, with its exquisitely hand-carved bannister.

It crossed her mind that being alone in an empty house—especially in the bedroom—with a man was not exactly the wisest move she'd ever made. Then she reminded herself that the man in question was Michael and nearly laughed at her strange feeling of uneasiness.

The rug on the stairs was faded, the pink roses nearly white. She thought of some carpeting she'd seen in the catalogue of Churchill's stock that would be absolutely perfect for here—a lovely cream Aubusson runner with a deep rose-colored border.

"Oh!" She stopped in the doorway Michael had indicated, staring in wonder at a room of enchantment, all glowing wood and cream walls.

A huge bed, with an intricately carved headboard and four graceful columns at least seven feet tall took up the center of the room. The sheets were ivory, trimmed with eight inches of exquisitely tatted lace. Lace that was echoed on the edges of the pillows strewn over the top of the bed, and on the windows, the latter cutting the slanting sun into golden diamonds that danced on the silk-draped walls.

"It's exquisite," she breathed. The bed, meant to be sunk into, reminded her of both the moss-stuffed mattress in the cabin Shayne had taken her to, and that marvelous fur rug.

"I'm glad you approve," a voice behind her murmured. A voice so much like Michael's, but not quite. She spun around, and found the object of so much of her recent misery standing in the doorway.

14

"WHERE'S MICHAEL?"

"He suddenly remembered a previous engagement."

"So he left me here. With you."

"I'm afraid so." Shayne walked a few steps into the room. "I was hoping, after you accepted yesterday's gift, that you might be ready to talk."

Bliss stepped backward. "That was a mistake." What on earth had made her keep those damn wind chimes?

"They're the same as the ones at the cabin." He kept walking toward her.

"You'll have to take them back." Bliss kept backing up until she was stopped by the mattress pressing against the back of her knees.

"Too late. They're yours now." He plucked a bright pink peony from a crystal vase on the brocade-draped table beside the bed. "Do you have any idea how much I've missed you?"

Not as much as she'd missed him, Bliss could have answered, but didn't.

"Okay, let's try another question," he said, when she didn't answer. "Do you have any idea how much I love you?"

They were the words she'd been wanting to hear for weeks. The words she'd dreamed of hearing more times than she cared to count. The words she was afraid to trust.

"Why should I believe that?" she asked. "After the way you behaved—"

"Abominably," he agreed. His eyes locked with hers, he closed the gap between them. "And it would serve me right if you never had anything to do with me again."

Heaven help her, he'd begun stroking her skin with the soft pink petals in a way that made her ache for the tender touch whose absence had tormented too many restless nights lately.

"That's what I should do." Bliss tried for cold anger, but knew that her shimmering sigh, as he trailed the blossom around her lips, gave her away.

"Probably." He watched her lips part and was struck with a sudden, almost overwhelming urge to crush his mouth to hers. But having waited so long for this chance to speak with her, Shayne didn't want to risk upsetting her. "But, before you do, may I give you one little word of advice?"

"What?"

"My mother has an old saying she used to tell us boys—about not cutting off your nose to spite your face."

"I know it," Bliss whispered. "Zelda says the same thing."

"I realize that I'll never be able to make amends for having betrayed your trust, Bliss. But if you give me a second chance, I promise I'll spend the rest of our lives making up for it. We're good together, sweetheart. Better than good, we're made for one another. Don't throw away your chance for happiness because you feel the need to punish me."

That was, of course, exactly what she'd been doing. She'd been miserable since finding out Shayne's true identity. And now, looking at his hollowed cheeks and the dark shadows beneath his grave blue eyes, she realized that she'd not been the only one suffering.

"How do I know you're telling the truth now?" she asked, deciding there was no point in denying how right they were for each other. "How do I know that as soon as I give you my heart again, you won't leave?"

"I'm working for Mike now," he reminded her.

"True. And before that you were working for Cunningham. You've spent your entire adult life roaming the world, Shayne. How do I know you're truly ready to settle down?"

"How about the fact that I bought this house?"

"You bought it? But I thought Michael..." She stared around the room, seeing it with new eyes, picturing the two of them spending lazy Sunday mornings in that magnificent bed.

"Oh," she said, as her gaze caught the chair in a shadowed corner of the octagon-shaped room. "Is that..."

"Raggedy Ann. You left her behind that day."

"I know." She'd missed the doll but had been too proud—and too stubborn—to ask for it back.

"I bought the house unfurnished," he revealed. "All I've bought so far is this bed, the table and that rocker."

"It's lovely. Where did you find it?"

"Lilah found it advertised in the paper."

"Lilah?"

"I don't know anything about antiques, so I told her what I was looking for and asked her to help."

"And she did. Just like that."

"She wasn't being disloyal, Bliss. She was only trying to help me win you back."

Bliss lifted a copper brow. "What makes you think that buying a rocker—and not even one from my shop— will make me decide to forgive you?"

"Because, although this conversation isn't going at all as I'd planned, I was hoping that you'd like the idea of rocking our babies in that chair."

"Babies?"

"I want to marry you, Bliss." He tossed the peony onto the bed and took her into his arms. "I want to make babies with you. Lots and lots of bright-haired babies with Spanish-moss green eyes and skin so smooth silk doesn't even come close."

He slipped a hand beneath her blouse and stroked her back, rekindling smoldering ashes. "I want to make those babies—and our life together—here in New Orleans, where we both belong.

"And someday, when we're old and gray, I want to watch you sitting in the rocker on the veranda of the cabin, while I teach our horde of grandkids how to catch crawfish for dinner."

"I suppose I'll be the one cooking all those crawfish to feed the hungry hordes." Her tone was dry, but the laughter in her eyes revealed she found the fantasy more than a little appealing.

"The kids will pitch in," he promised. "Because I'll be old and need lots of rest, so after all that hard work of crawfish catching, I believe a nap with Grandma would definitely be in order."

She laughed at that. "You're going to be a dirty old man, aren't you?"

It was going to be okay, Shayne realized. A cooling wave of relief flooded over him.

"You bet... What do you say, Bliss? I have an empty house that needs furniture. And love. And children. And I need a woman—the right woman, the only woman—to help me fill it with all those things."

Shayne O'Malley had lied to her, used her, made her the happiest woman in the world, then made her the most miserable. And now, looking up at him, Bliss realized that although she believed him when he said he loved her, life with this man would always be an adventure. The question was, was she brave enough to take it on?

"Bliss?"

He was still waiting for her answer. He'd waited long enough, she decided. They'd both waited long enough.

She twined her fingers behind his neck, her heart in her eyes as she smiled up at him.

"Yes. On one condition."

"Anything," he said without missing a beat.

Bliss knew he meant it.

"If we're going to have all those children, I think we should get started right away."

His laugh was expelled on a pent-up whoosh of relief. "Never let it be said I denied my woman anything."

As he pulled her down onto the bed he'd bought with her in mind, Shayne thought how ironic it was that after years of chasing adventure around the world, damned if he hadn't found all the adventure any man would need, right here in his own backyard.

And as Bliss's laughing mouth met his in a long, emotion-filled kiss, Shayne realized he'd finally come home.

*　*　*　*　*

Don't miss Michael's story
MICHAEL: THE DEFENDER, Temptation #654,
October 1997.

EVER HAD ONE OF THOSE DAYS?

TO DO:

☑ at the supermarket buying two dozen muffins that your son just remembered to tell you he needed for the school treat, you realize you left your wallet at home

☑ at work just as you're going into the big meeting, you discover your son took your presentation to school, and you have his hand-drawn superhero comic book

☑ your mother-in-law calls to say she's coming for a month-long visit

☑ finally at the end of a long and exasperating day, you escape from it all with an entertaining, humorous and always romantic Love & Laughter book!

ENJOY
LOVE & LAUGHTER™
EVERY DAY!

For a preview, turn the page....

"YOU'RE A VERY popular lady," Jed Kelley observed as Augustina closed the door on her suitors.

She waved a hand. "Just two of a dozen." Technically true since her grandmother had put her on the open market. "You're not afraid of a little competition, are you?"

"Competition?" He looked puzzled. "I thought the position was mine."

Augustina shook her head, smiling coyly. "You didn't think Grandmother was the final arbiter of the decision, did you? I say a trial period is in order." No matter that Jed Kelley had miraculously passed Grandmother's muster, Augustina felt the need for a little propriety. But, on the other hand, she could be married before the summer was out and be free as a bird, with the added bonus of a husband it wouldn't be all that difficult to learn to love.

She got up the courage to reach for his hand, and then just like that, she—Miss Gussy Gutless Fairchild—was holding Jed Kelley's hand. He looked down at their linked hands. "Of course, you don't really know what sort of work I can do, do you?"

A funny way to put it, she thought absently, cradling

his callused hand between both of her own. "We can get to know each other, and then, if that works out…" she murmured. *Wow.* If she'd known what this arranged marriage thing was all about, she'd have been a supporter of Grandmother's campaign from the start!

"Are you a palm reader?" Jed asked gruffly. His voice was as raspy as sandpaper and it was rubbing her all the right ways, but the question flustered her. She dropped his hand.

"I'm sorry."

"No problem," he said, "as long as I'm hired."

"Hired!" she scoffed. "What a way of putting it!"

Jed folded his arms across his chest. "So we're back to the trial period."

"Yes." Augustina frowned and her gaze dropped to his work boots. Okay, so he wasn't as well off as the majority of her suitors, but really, did he think she was going to *pay* him to marry her?

"Fine, then." He flipped her a wave and, speechless, she watched him leave. She was trembling all over like a malaria victim in a snowstorm, shot with hot charges and cold shivers until her brain was numb. This couldn't be true. Fantasy men didn't happen to nice girls like her.

"Augustina?"

Her grandmother's voice intruded on Gussy's privacy. "Ahh. There you are. I see you met the new gardener?"

It's hot…and it's out of control!

**This fall, Temptation turns up the heat
in select titles. Look for these bold,
provocative, *ultra-sexy* books!**

Available in September 1997:

NIGHT RHYTHMS by Elda Minger

Just a simple high school reunion—that's *all* it was
supposed to be for Meg Prescott. Until lean and sexy
Daniel Willett sauntered into the room. Together in the
dark of night they explored their deepest fantasies…and
hottest desires. But what would the morning bring?

BLAZE—Red-hot reads from

Take 4 bestselling love stories FREE

Plus get a FREE surprise gift!

Special Limited-time Offer

Mail to Harlequin Reader Service®

3010 Walden Avenue
P.O. Box 1867
Buffalo, N.Y. 14240-1867

YES! Please send me 4 free Harlequin Temptation® novels and my free surprise gift. Then send me 4 brand-new novels every month, which I will receive before they appear in bookstores. Bill me at the low price of $2.90 each plus 25¢ delivery and applicable sales tax, if any.* That's the complete price and a savings of over 10% off the cover prices—quite a bargain! I understand that accepting the books and gift places me under no obligation ever to buy any books. I can always return a shipment and cancel at any time. Even if I never buy another book from Harlequin, the 4 free books and the surprise gift are mine to keep forever.

142 BPA A3UP

Name	(PLEASE PRINT)	
Address	Apt. No.	
City	State	Zip

This offer is limited to one order per household and not valid to present Harlequin Temptation® subscribers. *Terms and prices are subject to change without notice. Sales tax applicable in N.Y.

UTEMP-696   ©1990 Harlequin Enterprises Limited

Let's Celebrate!

LOVE & LAUGHTER™

invites you to
the party of the season!

Grab your popcorn and be prepared to laugh
as we celebrate with **LOVE & LAUGHTER**.

Harlequin's newest series is going Hollywood!

Let us make you laugh with three months of terrific
books, authors and romance, plus a chance to win a
FREE 15-copy video collection of the best romantic
comedies ever made.

For more details look in the back pages of any
Love & Laughter title, from July to September,
at your favorite retail outlet.

Don't forget the popcorn!

Available wherever
Harlequin books are sold.

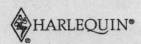 **HARLEQUIN®**

Look us up on-line at: http://www.romance.net

LLCELEB

HARLEQUIN WOMEN KNOW ROMANCE WHEN THEY SEE IT.

And they'll see it on **ROMANCE CLASSICS**, the new 24-hour TV channel devoted to romantic movies and original programs like the special **Romantically Speaking-Harlequin® Goes Prime Time.**

Romantically Speaking-Harlequin® Goes Prime Time introduces you to many of your favorite romance authors in a program developed exclusively for Harlequin® readers.

Watch for **Romantically Speaking-Harlequin® Goes Prime Time** beginning in the summer of 1997.

If you're not receiving ROMANCE CLASSICS, call your local cable operator or satellite provider and ask for it today!

ROMANCE CLASSICS

Escape to the network of your dreams.

Free Gift Offer

As Seen on TV!

With a Free Gift proof-of-purchase
from any Harlequin® book, you can receive
a beautiful cubic zirconia pendant.

This stunning marquise-shaped stone is a genuine cubic
zirconia—accented by an 18" gold tone necklace.
(Approximate retail value $19.95)

Send for yours today...
compliments of ◆HARLEQUIN®

To receive your free gift, a cubic zirconia pendant, send us one original proof-of-
purchase, photocopies not accepted, from the back of any Harlequin Romance®,
Harlequin Presents®, Harlequin Temptation®, Harlequin Superromance®, Harlequin
Intrigue®, Harlequin American Romance®, or Harlequin Historicals® title available at
your favorite retail outlet, together with the Free Gift Certificate, plus a check or money
order for $1.65 U.S./$2.15 CAN. (do not send cash) to cover postage and handling,
payable to Harlequin Free Gift Offer. We will send you the specified gift. Allow 6 to 8
weeks for delivery. Offer good until December 31, 1997, or while quantities last. Offer
valid in the U.S. and Canada only.

Free Gift Certificate

Name: _____

Address: _____

City: _____ State/Province: _____ Zip/Postal Code: _____

Mail this certificate, one proof-of-purchase and a check or money order for postage
and handling to: HARLEQUIN FREE GIFT OFFER 1997. In the U.S.: 3010 Walden
Avenue, P.O. Box 9071, Buffalo NY 14269-9057. In Canada: P.O. Box 604, Fort Erie,
Ontario L2Z 5X3.

FREE GIFT OFFER   084-KEZ
ONE PROOF-OF-PURCHASE
To collect your fabulous FREE GIFT, a cubic zirconia pendant, you must include this
original proof-of-purchase for each gift with the properly completed Free Gift Certificate.

084-KEZR